WolfWalkers

The Graphic Novel

Based on the film by
TOMM MOORE & ROSS STEWART

Adapted by
SAM SATTIN

Little, Brown and Company
New York Boston

About This Book
This book was edited by Rachel Poloski and designed by Ching N. Chan, Maria Caritas, Dwi Febri Novita, Dies Caya, Marsela Giovani of Caravan Studio. The production was supervised by Bernadette Flinn, and the production editor was Lindsay Walter-Greaney. The text was set in Jacoby, and the display type is Wolfwalkers.

Illustrations by Tomm Moore and Maria Pareja.

Cover design by Ching N. Chan.

Little, Brown and Company
Hachette Book Group
1290 Avenue of the Americas, New York, NY 10104
Visit us at LBYR.com/Wolfwalkers

First Edition: December 2020

Little, Brown and Company is a division of Hachette Book Group, Inc.
The Little, Brown name and logo are trademarks of Hachette Book Group, Inc.

The publisher is not responsible for websites (or their content) that are not owned by the publisher.

Library of Congress Control Number: 2020937579

ISBNs: 978-0-316-46178-8 (hardcover), 978-0-316-42953-5 (paperback), 978-0-316-42949-8 (ebook), 978-0-316-42951-1 (ebook), 978-0-316-42950-4 (ebook)

Printed in China

APS

Hardcover: 10 9 8 7 6 5 4 3
Paperback: 10 9 8 7 6

To the amazing wolf pack of artists and production staff who made the movie and this graphic novel possible.

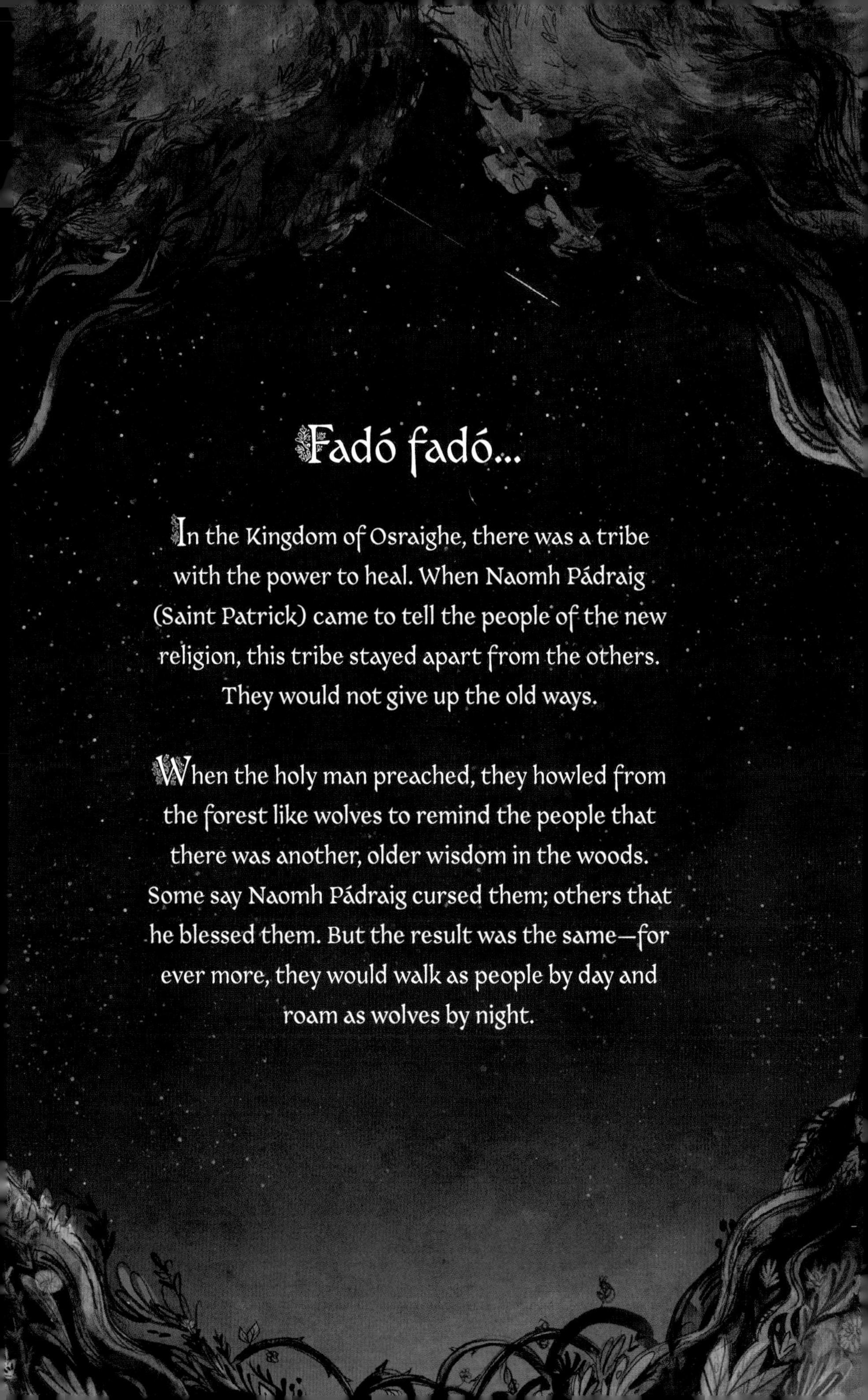

Fadó fadó...

In the Kingdom of Osraighe, there was a tribe with the power to heal. When Naomh Pádraig (Saint Patrick) came to tell the people of the new religion, this tribe stayed apart from the others. They would not give up the old ways.

When the holy man preached, they howled from the forest like wolves to remind the people that there was another, older wisdom in the woods. Some say Naomh Pádraig cursed them; others that he blessed them. But the result was the same—for ever more, they would walk as people by day and roam as wolves by night.

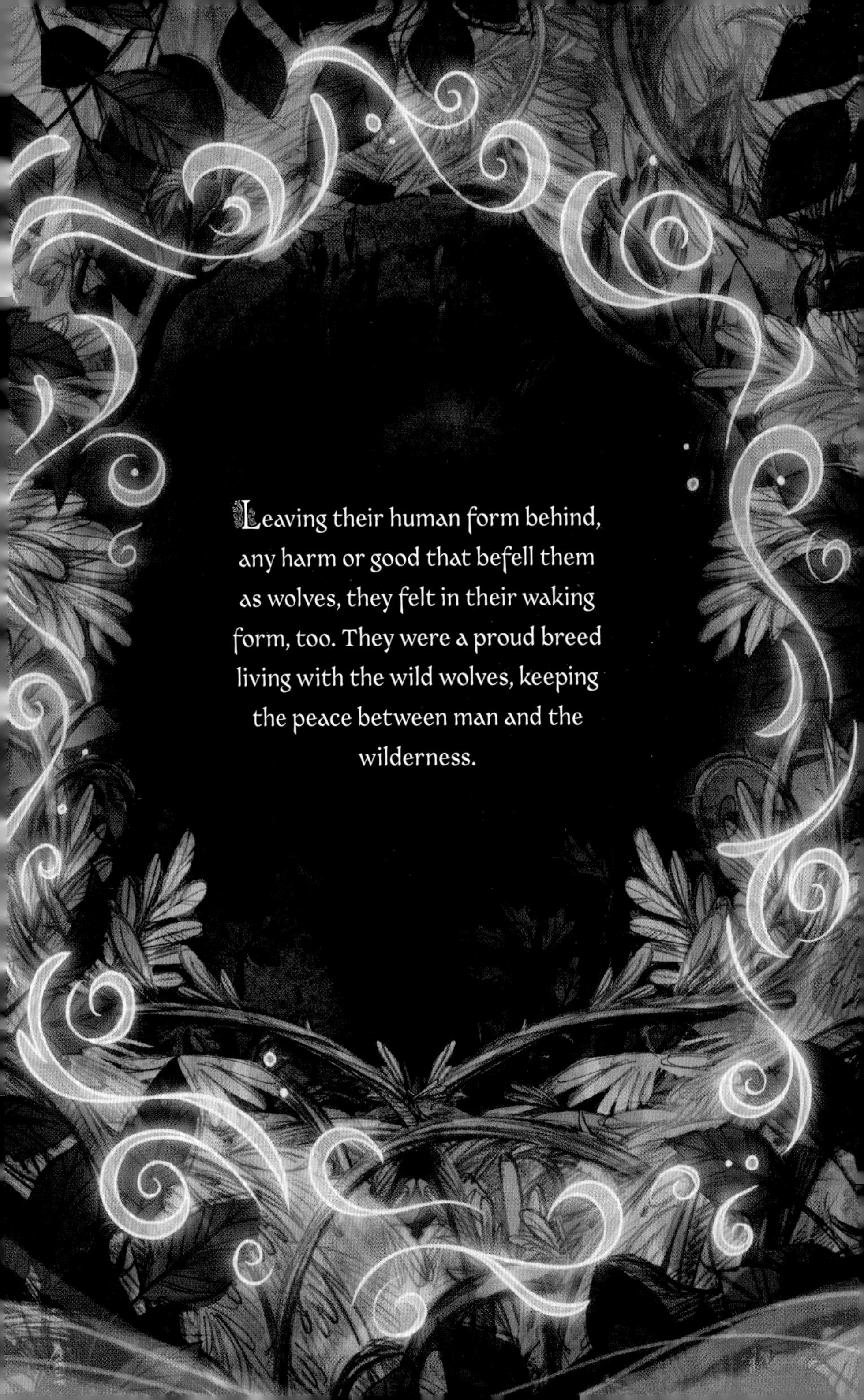

Leaving their human form behind, any harm or good that befell them as wolves, they felt in their waking form, too. They were a proud breed living with the wild wolves, keeping the peace between man and the wilderness.

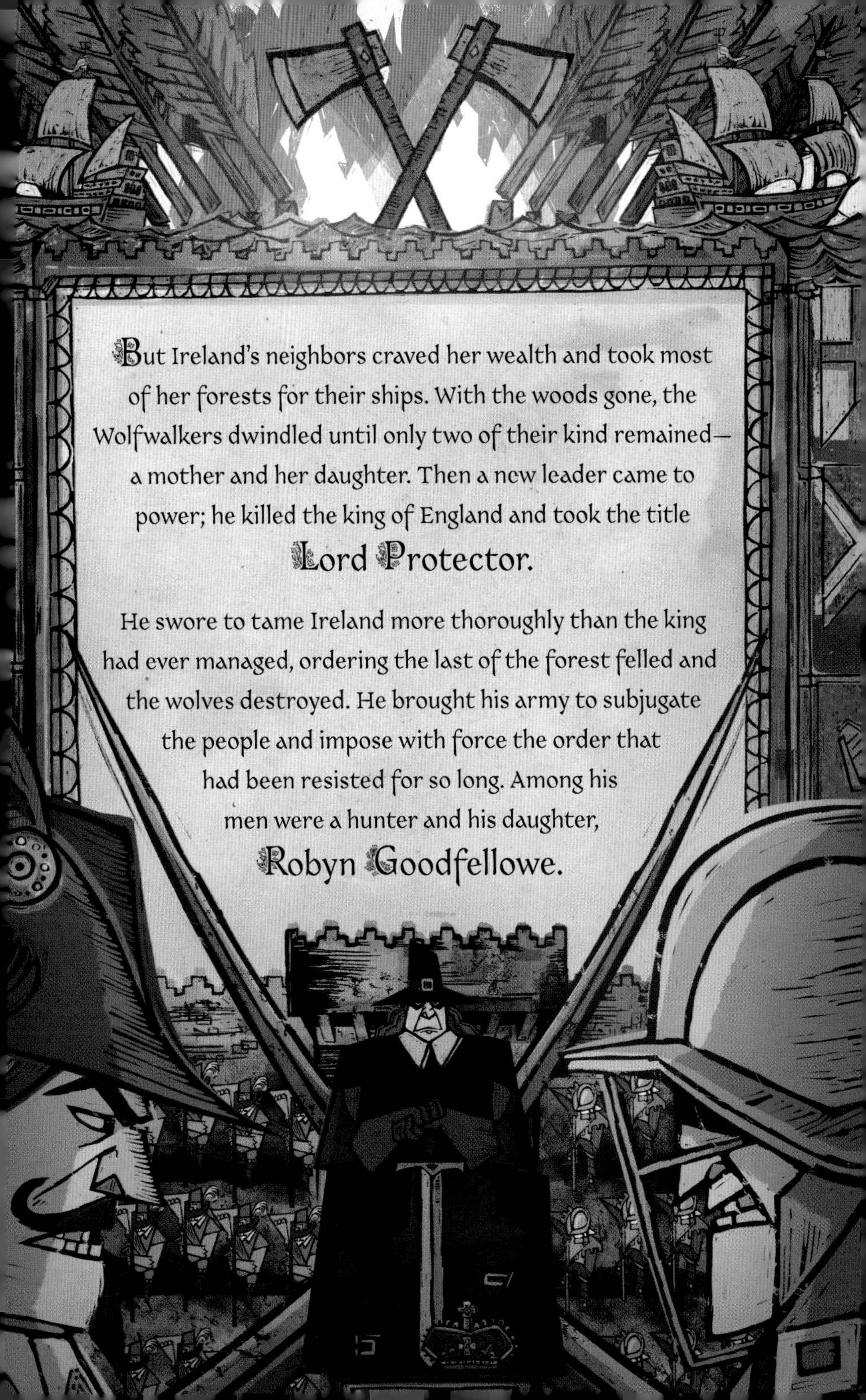
But Ireland's neighbors craved her wealth and took most of her forests for their ships. With the woods gone, the Wolfwalkers dwindled until only two of their kind remained—a mother and her daughter. Then a new leader came to power; he killed the king of England and took the title
Lord Protector.
He swore to tame Ireland more thoroughly than the king had ever managed, ordering the last of the forest felled and the wolves destroyed. He brought his army to subjugate the people and impose with force the order that had been resisted for so long. Among his men were a hunter and his daughter,
Robyn Goodfellowe.

CHOP!
CHOP!
CHOP!
CHOP!

CHOP!

GRRRRRR

Huh?

GRRRRRR

WOLF!

Get outta here, boys!
Watch out fer its bite!

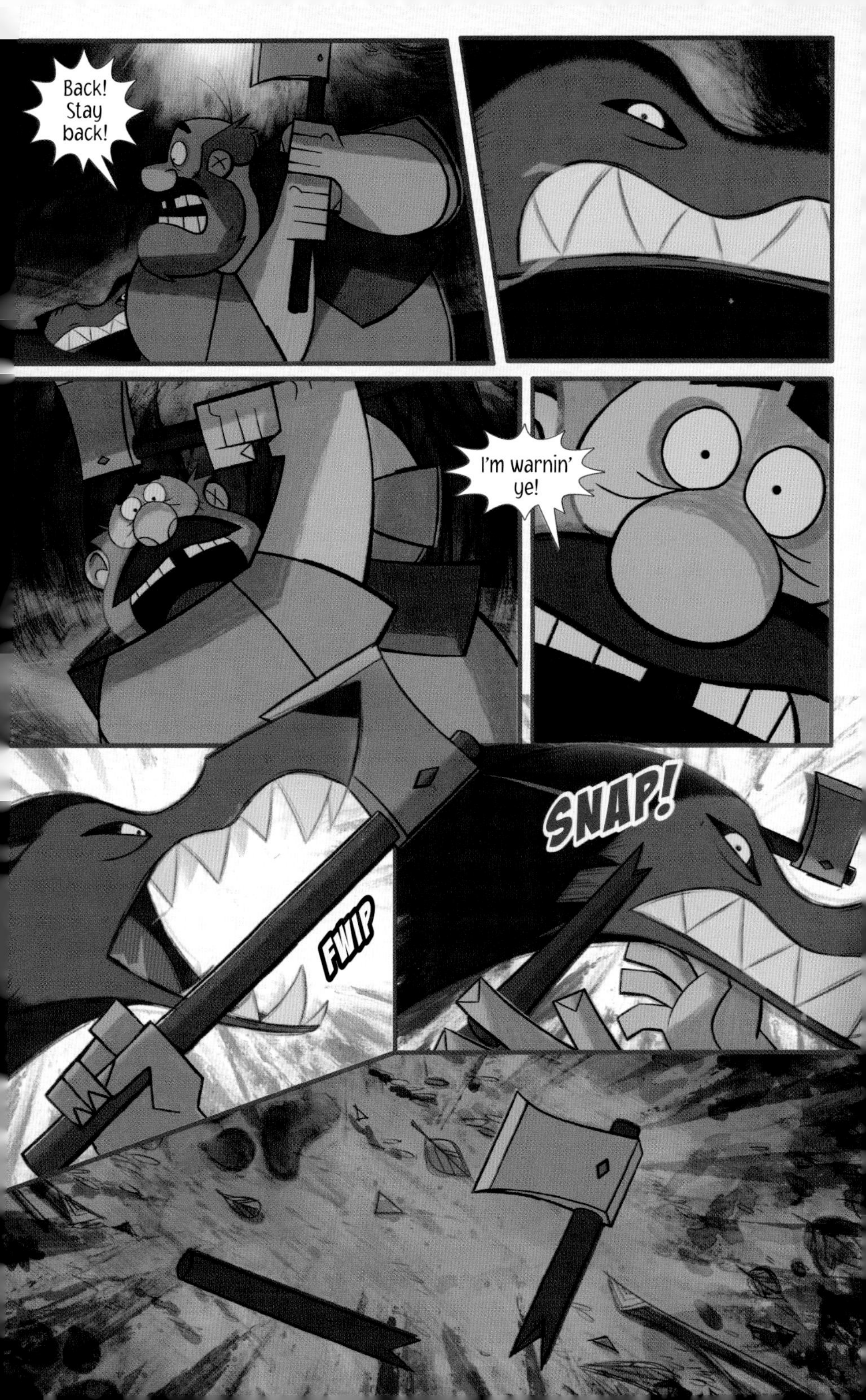
Back! Stay back!
I'm warnin' ye!
SNAP!
FWIP

GRAAR!
AAAAGH!
no!
GRRRR!

AWWOooo

Sweet Mother Divine, save us!

No...please...
I'm sorry....
Vhhhhmmmmmm

Wha... wha... **WHA...?**

Yer a...yer a **Wolfwalker?**

Go.
Th-thank ye.

BA-BONG!
BA-BONG!
They won't stop, love...these new invaders.

We need to get to the den!
Every day, they cut deeper into the forest. They'll keep coming until they find our den. And what do ye think will happen then?
I have to go find us a new place to live tonight.
I'm comin' with ye, Ma.
No, love. Ye have to look after the wolves while I'm gone. Yer a big girl now.
Remember to stay far away from the townspeople. I'll be back soon.
Do ye promise?
I promise, love.

Wolf, wolf,
kill the wolf.

Hunt them far
and yonder.

Wolf, wolf,
kill the wolf.
Till all the wolves
are done for.
TWOO

SHOO
WHUMP!
£5 REWARD FOR DEAD
WOLF
CHEEP!

You see that, Merlyn? Right on the nose.
Cheep?

Oh, come on! I was aimin' for the nose.

Cheep...
I'm glad you agree.

Robyn?!
Yes, Father.

Busy with your chores, I assume?
Why, yes, Father. Practically finished.
SWEEP SWEEP SWEEP
Well, it seems you certainly haven't been idle.
Pff. No way!
I've been sweepin' and dustin' and, eh...moppin'. Workin' so hard I can't keep up with myself!
I wonder what range that wolf poster is from here—
Fifteen feet?

No way. Twenty at least.
Hm?

What I **mean** to say is, I have no idea because, you know, cleanin'.

Robyn. This is our new home. The bucket and brush are your tools now.
Not this.
WOLF

WOLF
Ugh...It's **so** borin' bein' stuck in here all day.
I should be out on adventures with **you.** Like we did back in England.
Ah, lass... The Lord Protector has strict rules: no children beyond the walls. You know that.

The forest is brimmin' with ***real*** wolves, and it's my job to hunt them. Not yours.
I'm not afraid of a wolf.
You've never even seen a wolf!
I'm still not afraid of 'em!
That's why I must be afraid for you.
I'll just come with you to the gates.
I'll be back before sundown.
Stay indoors.

TUNK

Cheep.

Time to practice our trackin', Merlyn.
Cheep?
Yes! Now stop complainin'.

You track him. I'll follow.

Wolf, wolf, kill the wolf.
Hunt them far and yonder.
Wolf, wolf, kill the wolf.
Till all the wolves are done for.
Kill the wolf! Kill the wolf!

Get yer pickled oysters! Yer whelks and periwinkles! Wash 'em down with a cup of donkey's milk!

Yuk!

Oh, where's he gone?

Excuse me.
Pardon me.

Huh?

Robyn...

I was only goin' to track you as far as the gates.

Is that right? You weren't goin' to follow me out and slay a pack of wolves single-handed?
Well, yes! But only because I thought we could hunt them together. Wolves, bears—dragons, even!

What am I to do with you?
We could climb mountains and... and see giants!
Ha! You and your fanciful stories.
We could meet witches who cast spells, find mermaids...and selkies, even!
STOMP!
STOMP!
STOMP!
Goodfellowe! Goodfellowe! Come here a minute.

Yes, sir.

Stay here, lass.

Wolf! Wolf!

We've got the wolf! We've got the wolf!

Ha! Gotcha now, wolf...

Hey, English girl!
Where do ye think yer goin' dressed like tha'?

Like what? I'm a hunter. This is how we dress.
"I'm a hunter," she says. Would ye listen to her fancy-dancy accent?
I **am** a hunter! Just like my father.
He's the **best** hunter there is!
No, he's not. **My** father's the best hunter there is.
Yeah, well... **We're** huntin' wolves for the **Lord Protector!**
The Lord Protector, eh? He put me father in chains fer nothin'! Ye English think yer **sooo** great but yer **not!**
Ye should all just go home.
But first...

...give us a go on yer crossbow.
No way. It's mine.
Give it!
No!
Ye'll pay fer that, ***English girl.***
Wolf, wolf, kill the wolf.

Wolf, wolf,
kill the wolf.
Hunt them far
and yonder.
What's goin'
on here?

Soldier!
Leg it!

Why must you
wander off like
that, Robyn?

I was tryin'
to help! And then
there was a boy, and
he said his father
was better than you,
and then he wanted
me crossbow and
then—

Robyn, we are...not so welcome in this land yet.
You're better off to stay home while I'm workin'. It's safe there.
But I'd be just as safe out here with you.
No, Robyn! Stay inside. Do as you're *told.*
SLAM
Look, this evenin', when I'm back...
...you can help me make new arrows.
Then you can tell me your stories of giants and dragons.

Would you like that?

...I suppose so.
Great. Now then, be good.

If he could just see how good I am...

Chirp!

What a good hunter I am...

Then he'd ***have*** to let me come along.

Cheep?
What are you, Merlyn? A falcon or a chicken?

No children beyond the walls.
Lord Protector's orders.
...

Wolf, wolf, kill the wolf.
Hunt them far and yonder.
Hmm...
Wolf, wolf, kill the wolf.

TWOO!
Eh?
I got a flag, lads! C'mon.
Down with the Lord Protector!

You there!
Oi, stop this at once!
Get that flag!
Go on, ye little rebels!

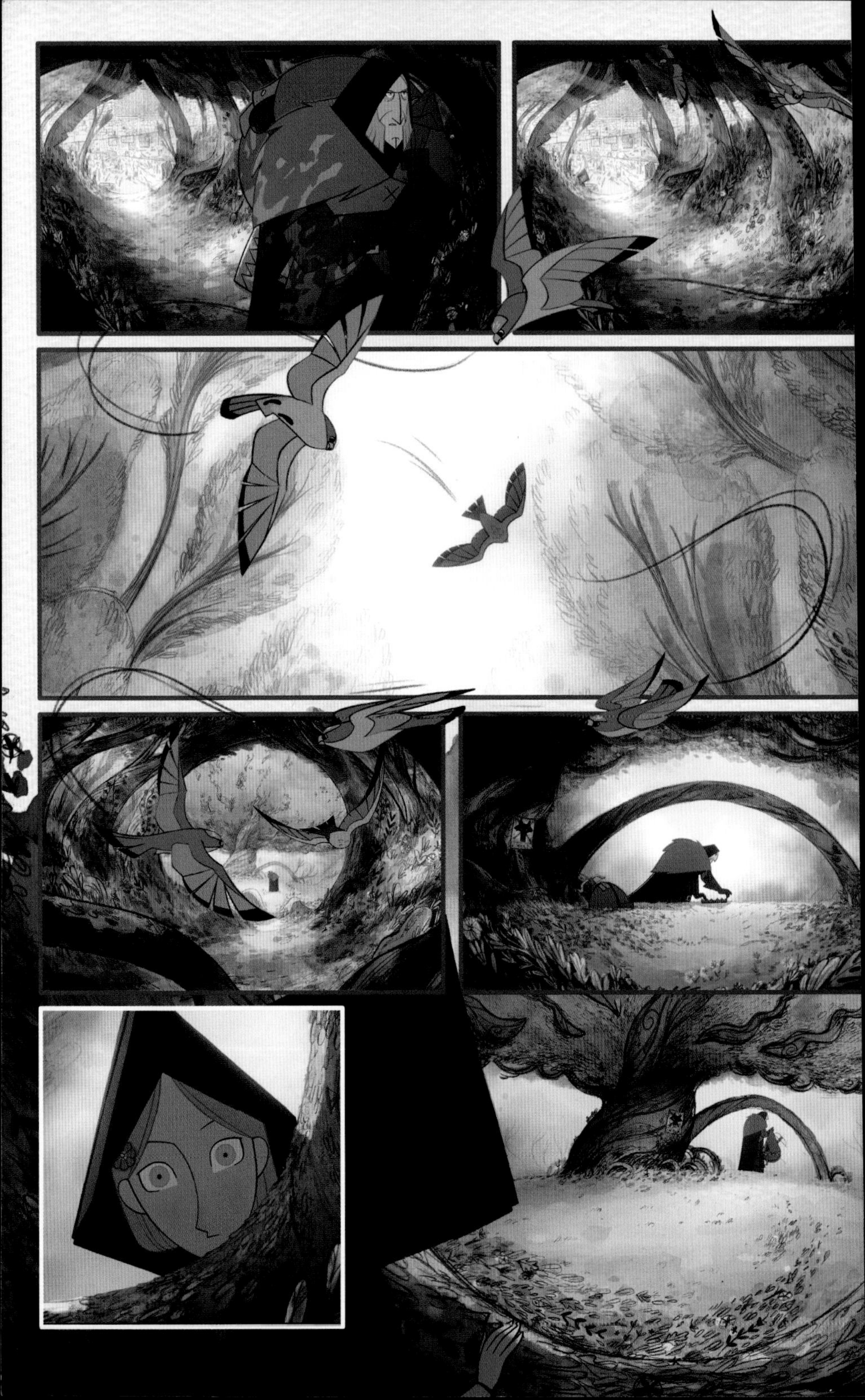

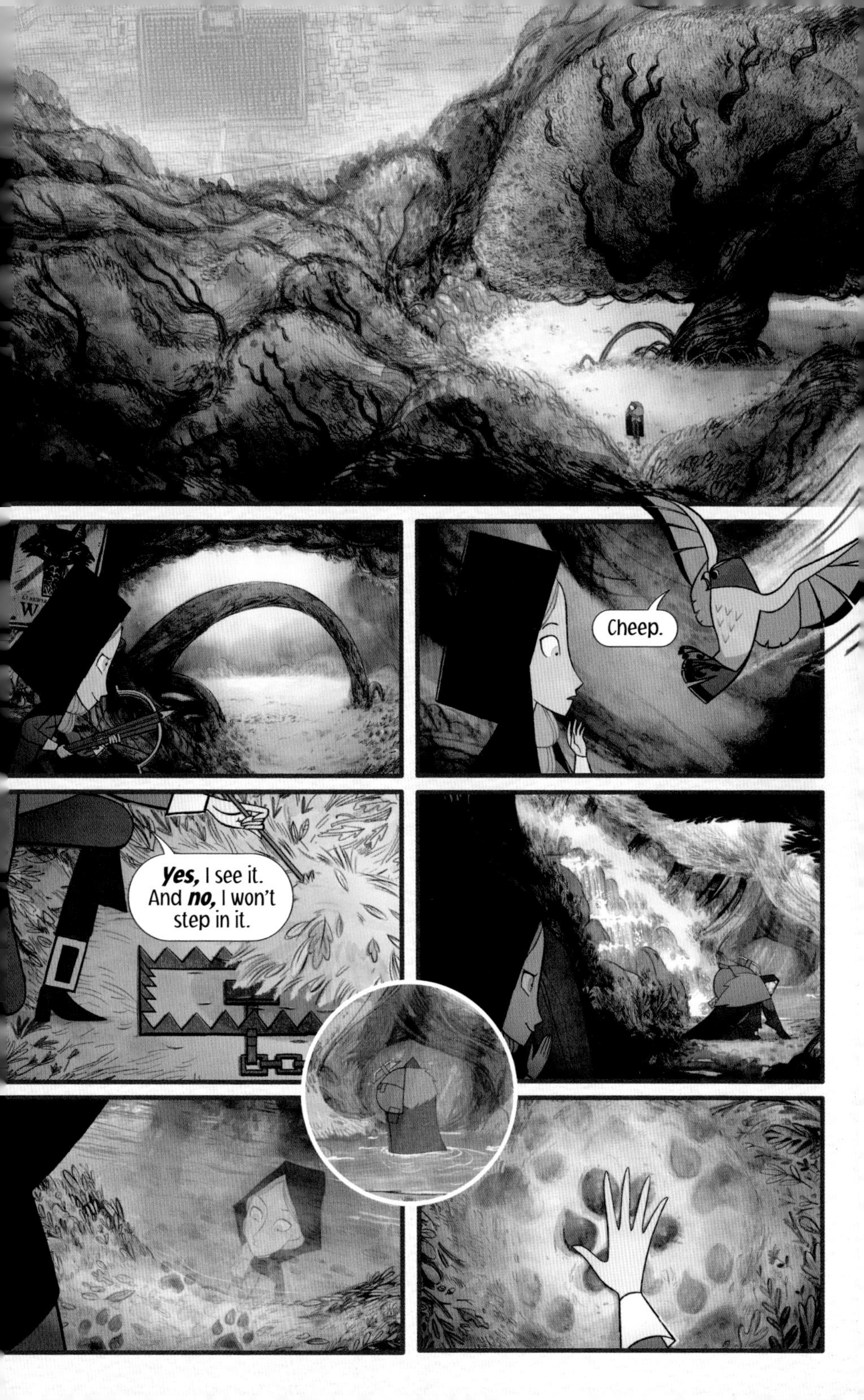
Cheep.
Yes, I see it. And no, I won't step in it.

DA-DING-DING-DING!
Help! Help! WOLF!
...Wolf?
Wolf!
Merlyn, quick! Find the wolf!
DA-DING-DING-DING!

CHEEEEP!
BAAAAAA!
BAAAAAA!
BAAAAAAA!
Wolf!
Get back!
Get back!
Help us!
GRRRAAAA...

Quick! Shoot! Fer God's sake, **shoot!**
GRAAR!
GRRRR!
TWOO!
UFFF!

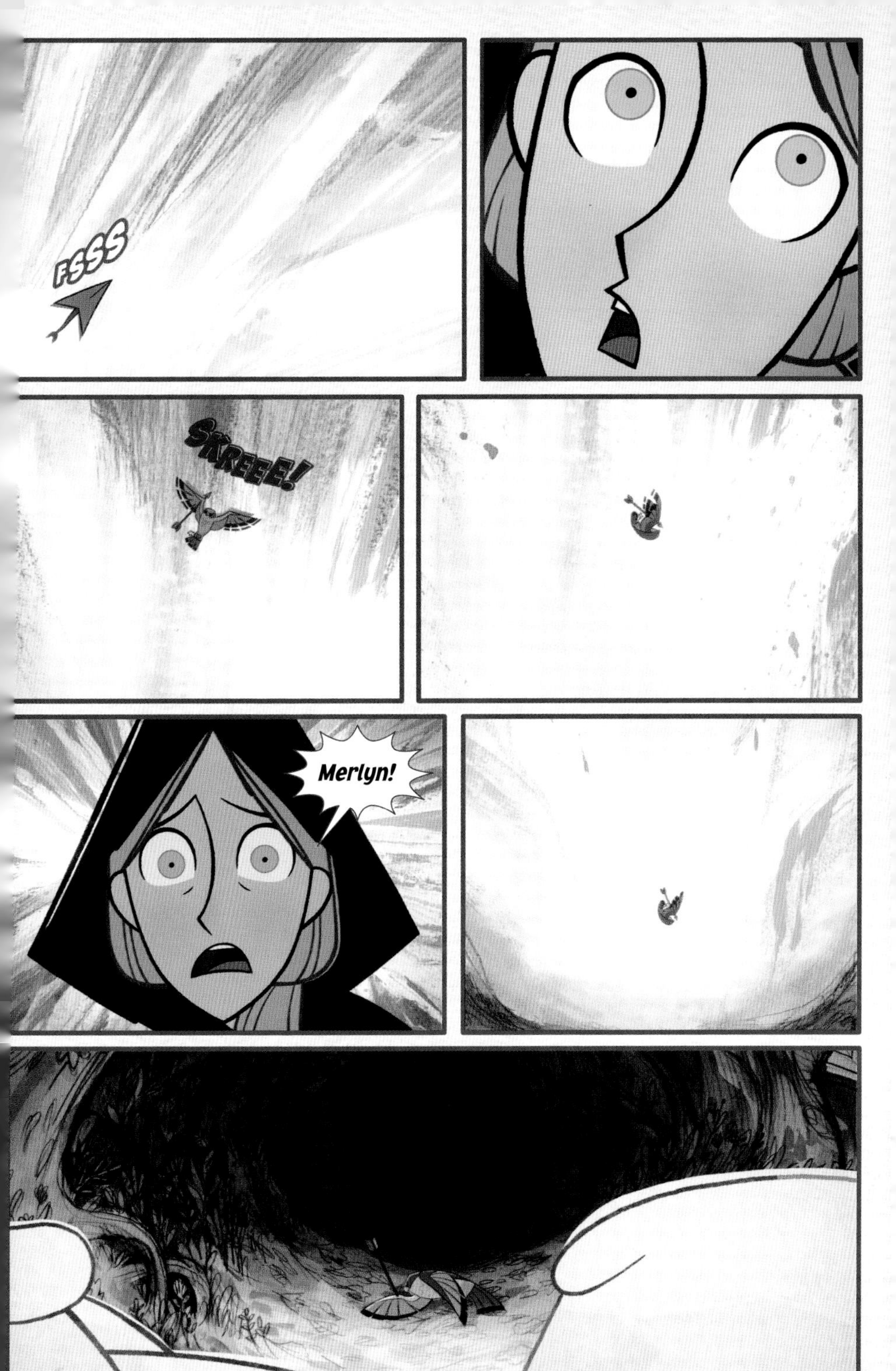
FSSS
SKREEEE!
Merlyn!

AWWOooo

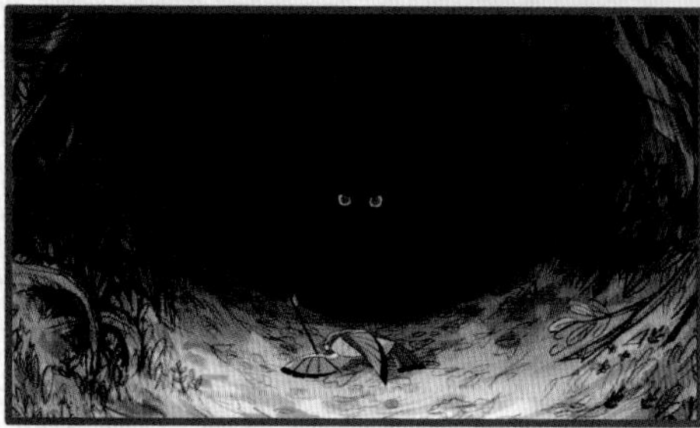

Hey! That's my bird. Leave him be!
Stop!
GRAR!

GRRRR!
FSSS
Yipe!
Wu-wu-wolves.
Over there.
Robyn!
AWWOoo
Robyn!

Robyn!
You could have been eaten alive! What were you thinkin'?
What are you *doin'* out here?
Merlyn! He's gone. We have to get him back!
No, lass. You're not goin' after him. Not out there.
But we can't leave him....
Robyn!
I promised your mother I'd keep you safe.
But...
It's OK, love. You'll be safe back in town.

By God, yer one lucky girl, ye know that?
'Twas a Wolfwalker. By Crom...

Now, calm down.

Everyone knows ye can't be cuttin' down their woods! If ye do, they'll get ya. Sure, ***that's the deal!***
There's no deal with anyone.

Saint Pádraig made a deal with the old pagans, and now yer breakin' it!
We need to clear the wood.
Did ye not see?
Actually, I did see the wolf attack.

The way them wolves answered her call?!

Them forests is ***riddled*** with wolves, I tell ye!

Well, it won't be long before the wolves are gone.
It won't be long before they're inside the town walls with the hunger.
No, we'll tame these lands. The Lord Protector has ordered it.
Ah...the great Lord Protector Cromwell... Renowned fer bein' so true to his word!
Hilarious.
snort
At least the old king kept us safe. This one? He's just an upstart. ***Lord Protector?!***
If you have grievances, you should speak with me directly.
Wha?! Now, I, eh...

I did nathin' wrong!

Another wolf attack?
Aye, my lord.
This is a joke! By Crom! The devil take yer head! May Pádraig drive ye back to England, ye snakes!

A few more like him and we'll have another rebellion on our hands.

If we don't clear the trees, the farmers cannot work the land.
And the woodcutters cannot clear the trees with these wolves.

This is not acceptable.
Aye, my lord.
We must show them the wolves are no threat. They're just beasts.
Finish them.
Yes, my lord.
That's your girl, yes?
It is, m'lord. This is Robyn.
There should be no child beyond the walls. Why is she not in the scullery?
M'lord... She doesn't work there.
You! See to it that the girl reports to the scullery.
Work is prayer, girl.

Father?
Do as the Lord Protector commands, lass.

I ride out to deal with a revolt in the south.
When I return I want all the wolves gone from this forest.
Yes, my lord.

You have two days.
Don't waste them.

Onward!

Hey. **Psst.** Girl.
The one who took yer bird. I seen her before—

A while back...with her ma. Cross me heart—she's one o' them **Wolfwalkers.**
Y'know, the ones that can talk to wolves like.
Sure, it's mad stuff, but it's true!

Wolfwalkers?

Yeah, they can ***heal*** as well. Her mother healed me with some wild magic.
Maybe she'll fix him up.
Or eat him... I dunno!
Merlyn... I need to get him back!
Well, I'd say once we're behind dem walls, neither of us is goin' anywhere.
Can you keep a secret?
A secret?
CLICK!

BAAAAAA!
BAAAAAA!
BAAAAAA!
BAAAAAA!
BAAAAAA!
BAAAAAA!
Wouldya lookit that, lads? Ye didn't lock that gate right at all!

Agh, me sheep!
BAAAAAA!
BAAAAAA!
BAAAAAA!
BAAAAAA!

Oi! Get 'im!
Ah sure, I'll get them!
BAAAAAA!
OI! Paddy! Mick! Whatever your name is! Get back in the cart!
BAAAAAA!
BAAAAAA!
BAAAAAA!
BAAAAAA!
BAAAAAA!
Here! Get down off that sheep.
These sheep are fast, eh, lads?
BAAAAAA!
BAAAAAA!
BAAAAAA!
BAAAAAA!

BAAAAAA!
BAAAAAA!
BAAAAAA!
BAAAAAA!

Now get back in there, you! An extra week in the stocks for that.
Where's the girl gone?
Oi, you two... look out for a girl. She ran into the forest. Get her and bring her back to the castle.

Lord Protector's orders!
Eh...yessir!

Damn English soldiers, who do they think they are? Bossin' us around...
What was that?
Nothin'!

Wolf, wolf, kill the wolf.
Hunt them far and yonder.
Wolf, wolf, kill the wolf.

FRSSSH

Merlyn...

Merrrrrllyn!

FRSSSH
FRSSSH

CHEEEEEEP!
Merlyn!

Look at you! You're...You're good as new, aren't you?!

I'm so glad you're not hurt. And your wing's all healed. How did ***that*** happen?

It was the girl, wasn't it?
Cheep!
What did she do?

I was afraid she was gonna eat you!
Chirp?
Oh, it doesn't matter. You're safe now.

Cheep?
Chirp!
Cheep chirp!

Cheep!
Huh?
Merlyn, stop that!
Stay back now. Back!
I'll shoot.
What the—?

WHOOOOSH
Oh...no...

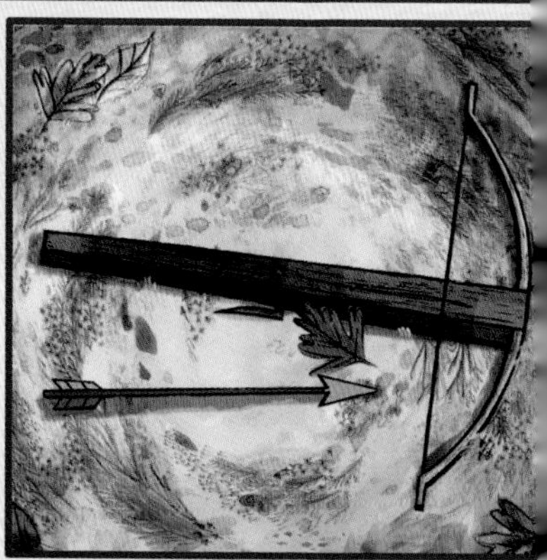

Get away, wolf! Or I swear I'll...
SNIFF
SNIFF
Go! Get away!
WHAM!

No! Get outta here!
Rar! Grf!
CHOMP!
GRRRRR!
SNAP!
Aggghhh!
WHUMP!

GASP!

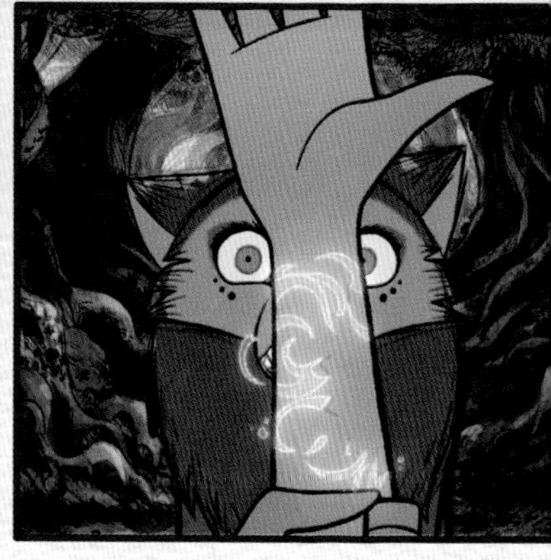

No. Get away...
Rff?

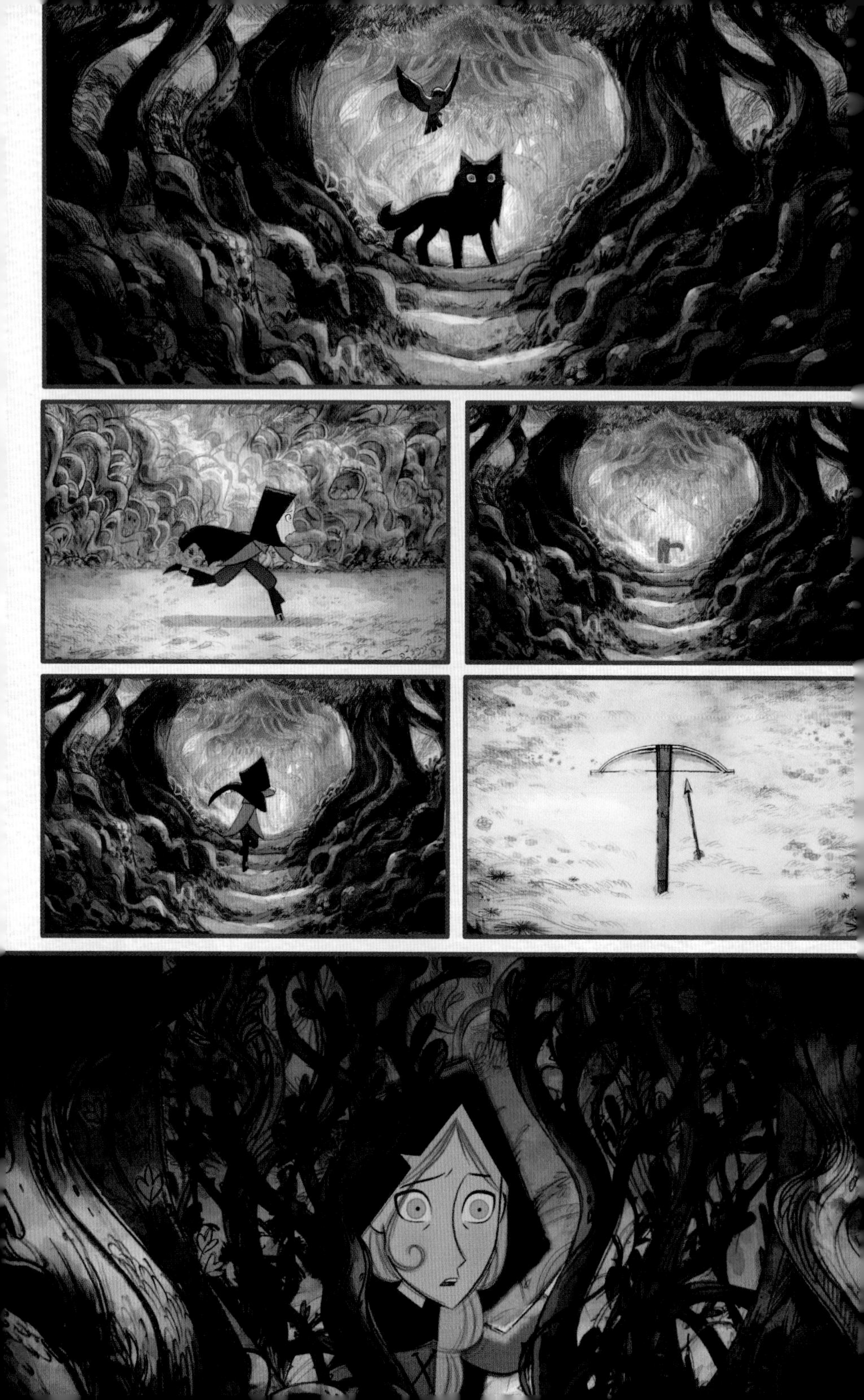

SKREE!

Merlyn!
Wait!

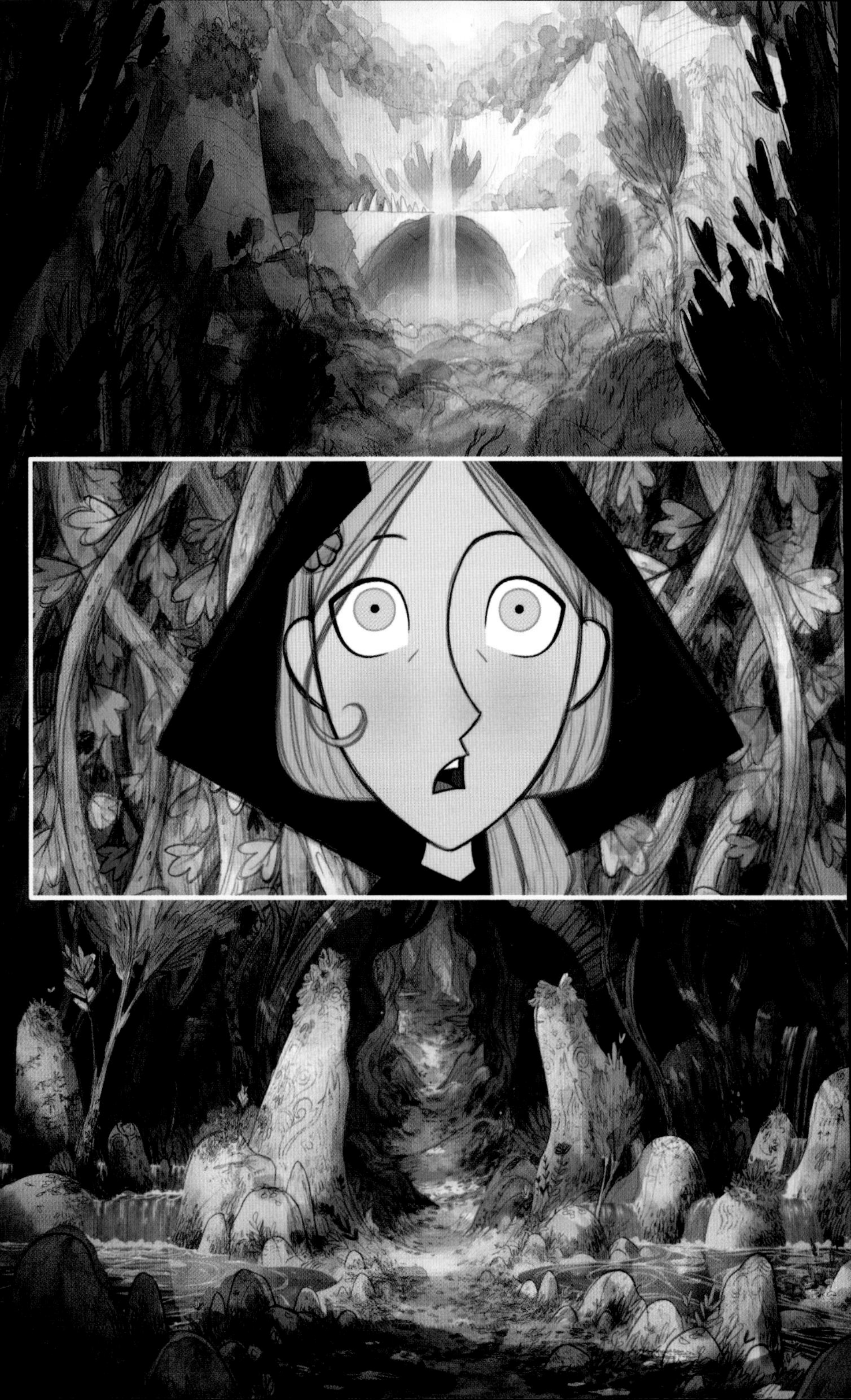

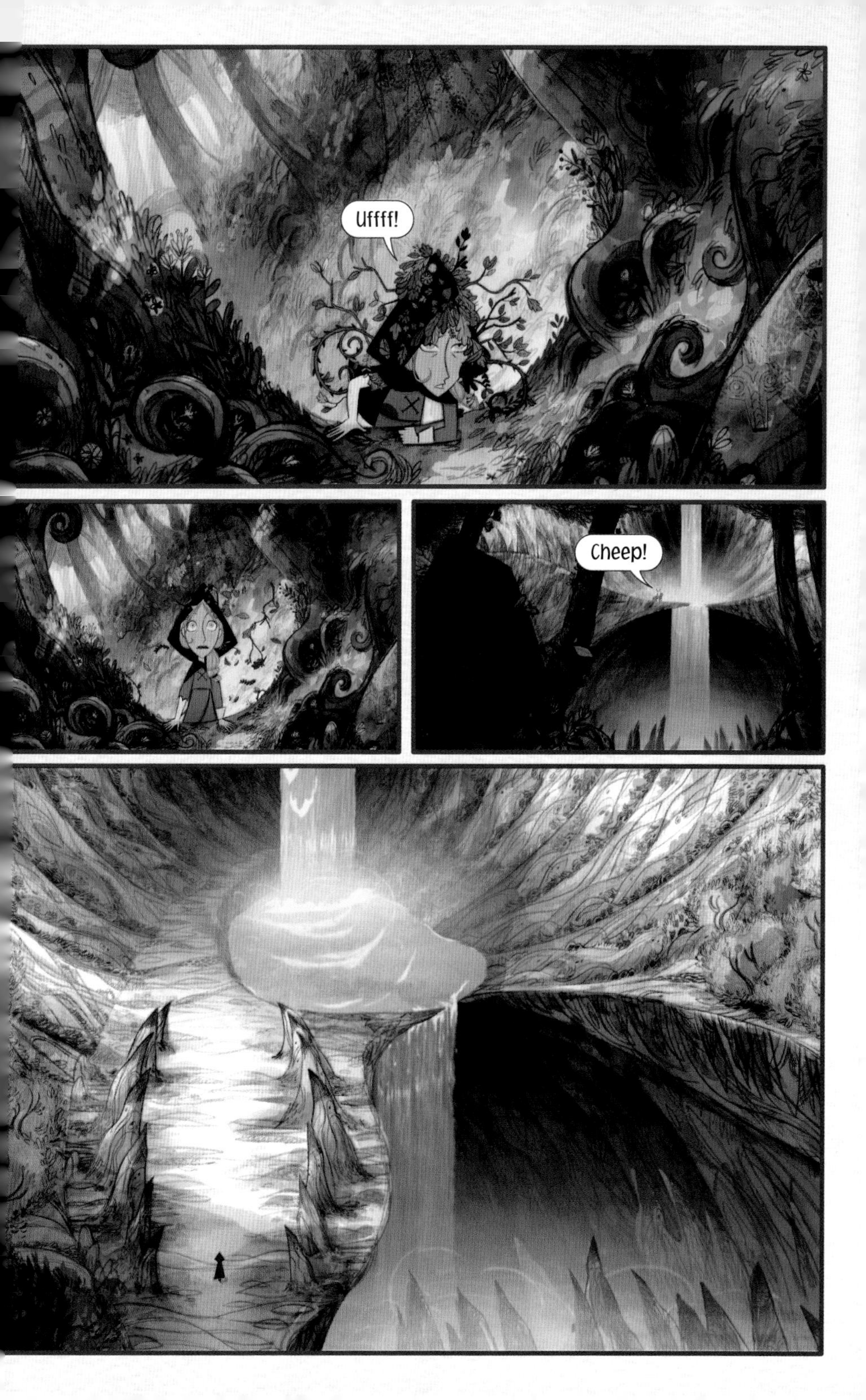
Uffff!
Cheep!

Whoa...
Cheep!

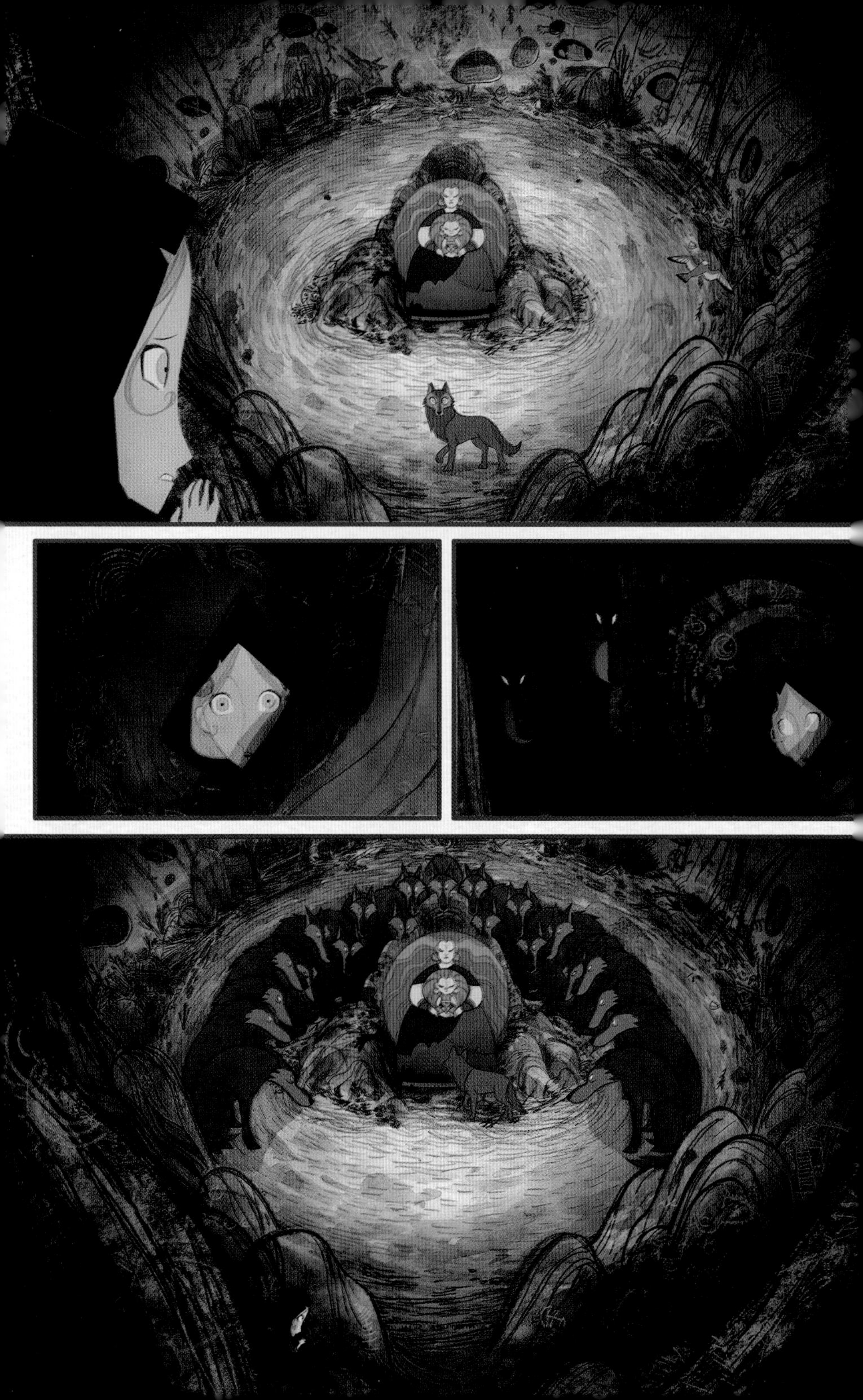

VHMMM

Wha...?

Ye can come out now. We can **smell** ye.
Yeah, ye **stink.** I knew ye were here the whole time...
Come out of yer hidey-hole. Let's see ye.
D-don't kill me.
Hah! I do what I like. Come here.
GRRRR!
You're a... you're a...
A **Wolfwalker?** So what?! Ye should thank me. I saved yer life!
Saved me?! You **bit** me!

Well, ye kicked me in the mouth enough times!
Well, you were attackin' me!
I was tryin' to get ye out of that trap.
An' anyway, ye came into **my woods.**
Your woods? These are ***our*** woods.
Your wolves are attackin' the woodcutters. And the sheep!
Well, they should be stayin' closer to the town. And so should ye, townie.

Now give us
a look at ye.

Are ye seein'
things?

Aggh!
Get **off**
me!

Stop it!
Yech!

Smells like
townie...Any
extra fur?

Hey, that's
mine!

Get off
me!

Will ye stop?!
Lemme fix it!

AWWOooo
AWWOoo
VHMMM
SHIMMER
SHIMMER
SHIMMER

Well, yer fixed now. Like nothin' never happened. Off ye go...
But...what... You ***did*** heal Merlyn, didn't you?
Yeah, I fixed ye and yer bird. Yer welcome, townie!
Now, ***bye!***
No, wait. Who's that? Is she your... mother?

...Ye better go or the wolves will eat ye.
But I don't...
Oh no! Too late! Now they're goin' to eat ye.

No!
Hah!
Cheep.
GRAAR!
Run away, townie girl. The wolves are after ye!

AGGHHHHH!
Get away from me!
But yer *so slow!*
All ye townies are slow. Except when yer tryin' to cut down the forest.
Scared o' yer shadows, ye are! Sure, what would a townie know about wolves?

Why do ye have so much stuff?
Hey, stop! That's me gear for huntin'.
Hunter?! Hah! A little girl like ya?
Well... you're a girl, too.
Up ye go!
I'm no girl. I'm a ***Wolfwalker!***
When I sleeps, I'm a wolf. When I'm awake, I'm me...
...Mebh!
Mebh Og MacTire!
RAWR!

What's yer name anyway?
Robyn.
Robyn, eh? I like birdies.
Always cheepin' and skittin' around the place. Kinda like me—
Except I can't fly...
Well, I can jump really high, but not as high as a robin....
Watch out!

SNAP!
AAAAGHHH!!

Caught again? Some hunter...

That's **two fer me, none** fer ya!

Stop bein' so **annoyin'.** It's not funny, you know.
UGGGH. LET. ME. DOWN!
Alright, townie, if ye say so!

SNIP
Stop! No! Wait!
WHUMP!
Yech! That's enough. Call them off.
Alright, townie.
Stop callin' me townie!
Alright, **Rooob-bynnn.** Fun's over. Back home wi' ye.
Well, Mebh Óg Mac-a-Tin-er-reh, your idea of—

Shhh...D'ye hear that?
Mmph?
A man. I'll get rid of him.
A man?
Oh no... Father.
Grrr...

FSSSHHH
Just one townie. I'll give him a bit of...
...a scare.
no...
ye..!

Huh...

BRSSSH

That was too close.

What are ya so scared of? We have a **pack o' wolves** with us!

WHAM

Hey! I told ye! **Ye can't go out in the daytime.** Ma said so.

Go back to bed!

Is that your ma back in the cave?
Of course! Sure, don't I look like her?
Are any of the other wolves, uh, people?
Nooooo... Jaypers, are ye mad?
How big d'ye think me family is?

I'm not supposed to be out here. Listen, I've got to get back.
Great, I'm mad to get rid of ye. Close yer eyes.
What? Why?
I don't want ye comin' back to me den. It's secret.
But... I already found it.
Oh, just shut up and walk. I'll point ye back to the town.

I need my crossbow back first.
What do ye need that fer? Shootin' yer bird again?
No. Shootin'... oh...never mind.

Hey, stop pushin' so fast.
Oh, will ye stop complainin'?
So, what's it like? You know, bein' a wolf?
Hmm...It's great. Ye see different... smell different.
Hear different.
And how did you fix Merlyn's wing—and my wound?
I can heal things. I'm a Wolfwalker. Don't ye know anythin'?
I know you need a bath.
Smell that?

Uuuuggh, Mebh...?
Town tasties.
Town tasties?
Where's she gone now?
Oh no.
Damn soldiers, Ned...What did ye tell them?
Just she's gone home, isn't she? 'Tis obvious.

But, Ned. Say if that wolf bit her. That means she could turn into one of them.
A wolf?
...Wolfwalkers?! Hehe. Would ye stop?
No. One o' dem half wolf, half witch, half people!
We're cuttin' down their woods, Ned. Shouldn't be doin' it.
Save me that nonsense. The soldiers are makin' us...
...but if old Lord Ironsides doesn't sort out those wolves, it won't just be us who'll stop takin' his orders.
No more orders fer me, Ned!
He'll have to turn tail back across the water.
Away home with him, Ned!

We'll wave him goodbye.
And we won't be letting no stuck-up lord into our city again!
Not me, Ned!
No, we won't, Ned!
The Lord Protector can go protect some other city that needs no protectin'!
My crossbow...
He can—so he can, Ned!
Those are mine.
Huh?
Those town tasties are mine.
I'm not after those. I need my crossbow back.

Eh? What?
What is it, Ned?
The wind, maybe? What did ye do with the spuds?
The spuds, Ned? Hey! The bread's gone, too!
No spuds and bread! Me **hat!** Give it back!
Me bread! Gimme that!
No! Gimme me hat!
Wait! There's someone in there....

Me milk! Somethin' took me milk!

Haha! They nearly caught us.
BURP!
SNAP
Nobody can catch me, townie.
How can ya stand livin' in there? All the smells... Ugh!
SIGH
It is pretty smelly. I don't like bein' stuck in there...I miss England.

What's an England...?
I used to live there...
I could go where I wanted, play with me friends...
It was really nice.
Merlyn and I used to even help Father hunt for food.
Nom nom nom!
Stay here in the forest. It's great! Loads of runnin'...
...Playin'...
...Eatin', messin', climbin'...
...Free.
I can't...I can't leave my father.
He has to work for the Lord Protector and...
Mebh! You can't stay in the forest, either!
They're cuttin' it all down!

No way! I'll **scare** them off!
The Lord Protector wants the wolves gone. Dead! You have to leave.
We **were** leavin'. Me, Ma... with the pack.
What stopped you?
Ma went off....
As a wolf?
Yeah... to find us a new place to live.
I'm sure it's some **huge** den with no stinkers around. And **loads** of food.
It's goin' to be **amaaaazin'.**
So then... where is she?
Do you think she got caught?
She's fine! **Nobody** can catch **my** ma! And anyway... if she was caught by those stinkers, I'd get me wolves to **ate them!**

So...you're waitin' for her to come back?
Yep. It's just her and me in the whole world.
Like me and Father...
But what if they find the den?
No. They won't. Nobody has.
Well, I did.
Yeah, only cos I let ye.

RARRRRRR
BAAAAAA!
BAAAAAA!

I have to tell my father about you.

He didn't know...
SNAP!
We didn't know that Wolfwalkers were real... That you were people.

I better get back.
Pbbbbth.
Look, I'm goin' to help you. Wait for me at the big tree tomorrow.
I'll bring you some bread—
I mean, some town tasties.
Nom nom nom!
Alright so, smell ye later, townie!
Not if I smell you first! Ha!

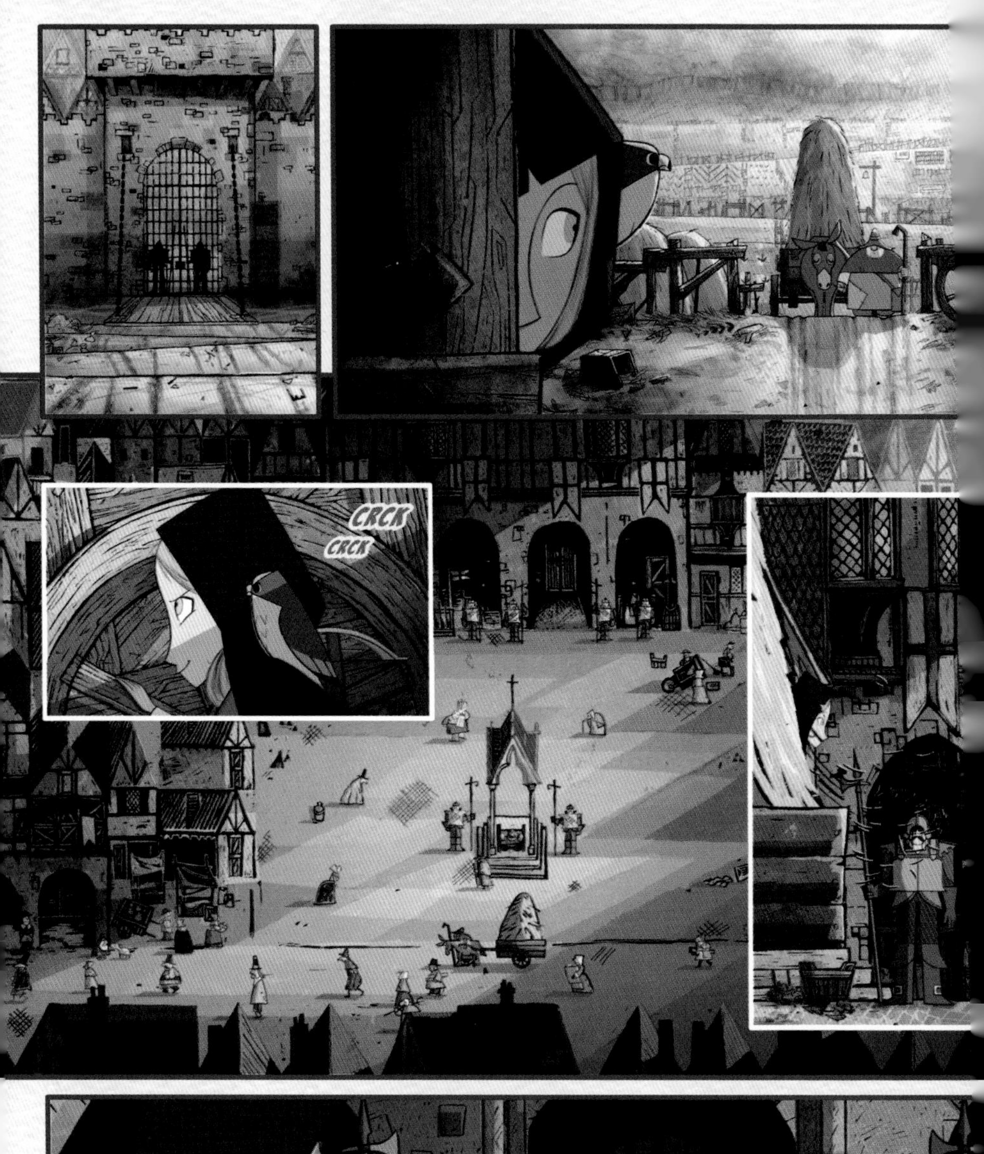
CRCK
CRCK

'Tis yerself!
Sure, they didn't eat ye, eh? That's great.
You were right...
That girl **healed** Merlyn!
And I met her.
Didn't she now? I told ye.
She's actually really nice when she's not tryin' to eat you!
I better get back....
Ye know where to find me, anyways, if yer lookin' fer me!

Father? Father?
We need to tidy this place up before he gets back.
"My, Robyn. This place is sparklin'."

Thank you, Father, take a seat. Put up your feet.

"Don't mind if I do, lass."

Hard day huntin'?
"Aye, not a sniff of wolf out there."

Well...what if I told you I can get all the wolves to leave and we don't even have to kill them?

"I'd say you're tellin' tall tales again."

Oooh, but I'm not.

Now, promise me you won't get angry....
"I promise."

You see, I met a girl in the forest who has magic healin' powers. She healed Merlyn. And she's a ***Wolfwalker.***
"A Wolfwalker?!"
It's true. When she sleeps, she turns into a wolf.
She can talk to the wolves. Smell and act like them, too. Her and her mother were goin' to take the wolves away, but her mother went missin'.
"Missin'? Poor thing."
I know, but if we can help her find her mother—
then they can all leave the forest together and you will have done your duty to the Lord Protector.
"Oh, brilliant, lass. Absolutely brilliant. Thank you. Our problems are solved."

We can go back to how things used to be—
CLICK
CREEEAK

Ah, my girl. Come here to me.

Are you alright? How are you after that wolf attack? A bit shaken?
No, I'm fine. Take a seat. Put up your feet.
Ahh, that's nice. And how was your scullery work? You must be tired, love.
Well, about that—
And you still managed to clean the house!
What if I told you—
And Merlyn is back! My, you've had quite the day, lass.
Yes, I have, but what if I told you—
My day has been awful.
Every trap I set this week has either been broken or sprung.
Never seen the like of these wolves!
Father...what if I told you I can get all the wolves to leave and you don't even have to kill them?
Now, promise you won't get angry with me.

Go on?
You didn't promise.
I know. Go on.
You see, I went back to find Merlyn—
You were out in the woods?!
You went back?!
Father, listen, she's one of them. A Wolfwalker like the woodcutter said! They're real!

But, Father—
You left the scullery?
Well, I didn't actually get to the scullery—

What?! The Lord Protector ordered—
If we just find her mother and—
You *have* to follow the Lord Protector's rules! He gave you a direct order, and you disobeyed him.

Have you no fear of the stocks?
We need to work together to stay in this town, lass.
I'll bring you to the scullery tomorrow myself.
Please, I thought you would understand...
I...I can help you. If we just—
Help me by doin' your work and stayin' in town.
Away from danger. Now promise me.
I promise, Father.
Now go to your bed.
She would have wanted you safe, Robyn.
Mother would have listened to me.
Sleep well.

We'll find a way to help her, Merlyn.

AWWOooo
PANT
PANT
PANT

VHHHHHMMMMMM
Wahh!

Robyn?
Father?

Are you alright?
It's nothin'. Just a bad dream.

Well, should make an early start of it.
Both of us. Let's go.

CLATTER
CLATTER
CLATTER
WHACK
WHACK
Oh! Nice to have a new girl joinin' us.

Keep an eye on her. She's to work the full day.
Remember, Robyn. Work is prayer.

'Tis alright, child. I was only half yer age when I started here. Just do as yer told now and ye'll be grand.

BRSSH
BRSSH
RUB
RUB
STIR
SCRUB
SCRUB
CLATTER

How...?

Work is prayer, girl!
Better if ye don't stop.
SPLSH
Oh no!

CLICK
Huh?
GRRRR...

Grrrrl...
Girl...
What in the world?! Get yerself out of this room, girl!
The Lord Protector has forbidden *anyone* from enterin'.
Sure 'nuff I thought I had the door locked.

Yer lucky 'tis me that found ya, child, not his lordship.
Put ye in the stocks, he would.
The Lord Protector expects his rules to be followed.
Remember that tomorrow.
Now, off hom
with ya.

Ah now, there ye are.
Did ye see yer new friend again?

No, I can't get out...I have to work in the castle...

I think...I think I heard—
Robyn!

Come in!
You will catch your death out there!

Well, now. Are ye a hunter or a housemaid?
SLAM
Work is prayer, Robyn.
Then I prayed the whole Bible.

Good lass.

This is still new for you.
It is a righteous life for a young lady.
Well, it's no life for me!

I can get the Wolfwalkers to leave.
You just need to listen t' me—

Robyn Goodfellowe, enough of your stories.
I can go look for her—

You must do as you're told! No more fairy tales!
But—

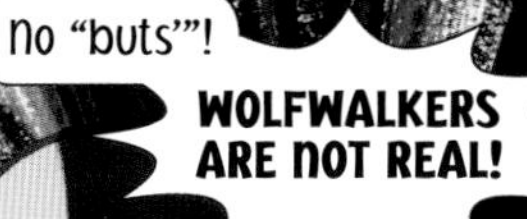
No "buts"!
WOLFWALKERS ARE NOT REAL!

Now go to bed.

They *are* real...
Right, Merlyn?
Chirp.
AWWOOOOOO
SNORE

AWWOOOOOO

Ungh.
DA-DUMP
VHHMMMM
DA-DUMP
DA-DUMP
DA-DUMP

Huh?
Merlyn...
Cheep.
Can you... smell that?
Gasp!
Chirp cheep CHIRP!
Merlyn, what's happened to you?
I can...***see*** your scent....
What?!

CRSSH!
Father!
It's—it's me.
Whuh!

Rff ruff grrr
WHOMP!
No, no! Father!
It is me!
FSSS!
THWACK!

Robyn!

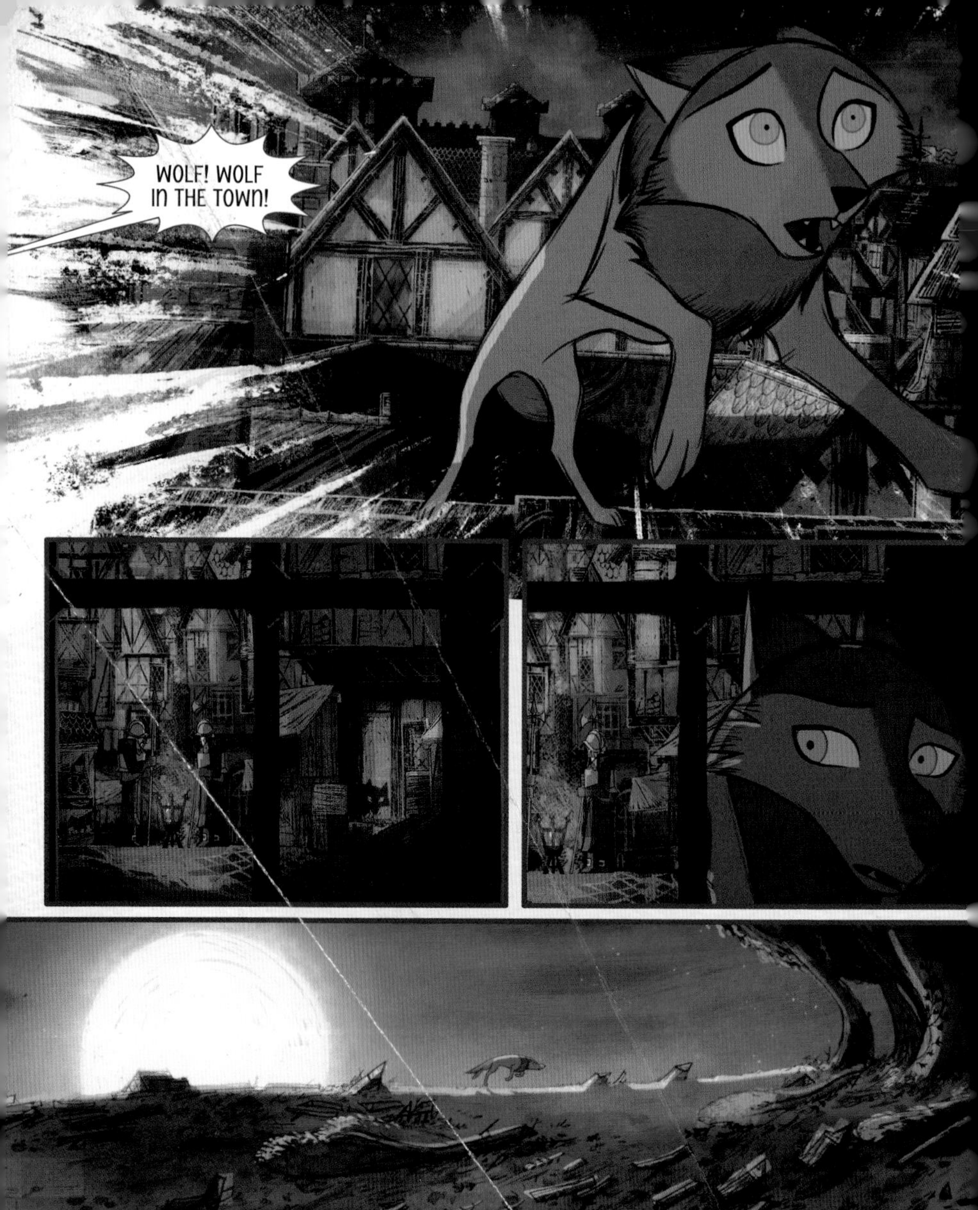
WOLF! WOLF
IN THE TOWN!

I'm not scared.
I'm not scared.
CRSSH!
Mebh?

Mebh!
Mebh!
Mebh...
Mebh?!
CRRRSSSSHH

Mebh...
GRRRR!
Robyn!
Something's happened to me.

Yeah, I can see that!
Ooooh... thought I'd fixed the bite.

I thought ye'd be fine... Ma's goin' to **kill** me!

Well, my father **will** kill **me!**

SNF
SNF
Hey! Calm down and give her room.

WHIMPER
WHIMPER
Go back to bed!

Now I see ye like this, it's flippin' great.
I thought we were the last ones.

It's *great?!* I'm a ***Wolfwalker!***
I know! Ma said this would be bad.

Like, never to bite anyone...but...I ***love*** it! It's smashin'!

This is bad. I'll get killed like this. What about my body?
It's asleep, nice and cozy. Look...

...yer a wolf when ye sleep.
A girl when yer awake.

No big deal!

But the soldiers.
And—and my father...

Don't worry about that.
Learn how to be a wolf first! Come on!

Why do ye ***want*** to be a human?
Bein' a wolf is ***way*** better. I'll show ye.

Can ye smell me?
Of course! Everybody can!

Haha! Well, close yer eyes.
Ye don't **need** yer eyes to see!
"And ye can hear ***every little thing*** that moves!"
TUMP
TUMP
TUMP
"And yer paws can ***hear*** through the earth..."
TUMP
"And ye have four legs now!"

Hey, wait for me!
"Keep yer nose down!"
"Ye can run really fast and jump so high!"
"Be a wolf!"
HAHAHAHA!

You let them out?
The forest is ***ours*** at night. Wait till ya see!

AWWOooooo

Well, townie, this is as far as we go.
The woods are gettin' smaller every day.
I know.
I try and scare them off—**RARR!**
But they just don't get it!

How about tha'?
A lot of smelly people there.
Hey—I'm in there.
Fast asleep, snorin' away...
Whew. I better go back...
I'm scared, Mebh.
Yeah... Town's no place fer a wolf...

I know. If they don't shoot me, they'll cage me.

Mebh, your mother...Do you think that they might've—
No!

Nobody can catch **my** ma.
Sorry.

How long has she been gone?

Since...
She's all right. She'll be back soon.... She promised.

Well, don't worry. Wherever she is, we'll find her. I can help you.
Yeah! There's two of us now!
I'll sneak out and meet you back here tomorrow.
I'll be waitin' fer ye! ***Again!***
Mebh, we'll find her. Then you can all leave. And be safe.
Ye promise?
I promise.

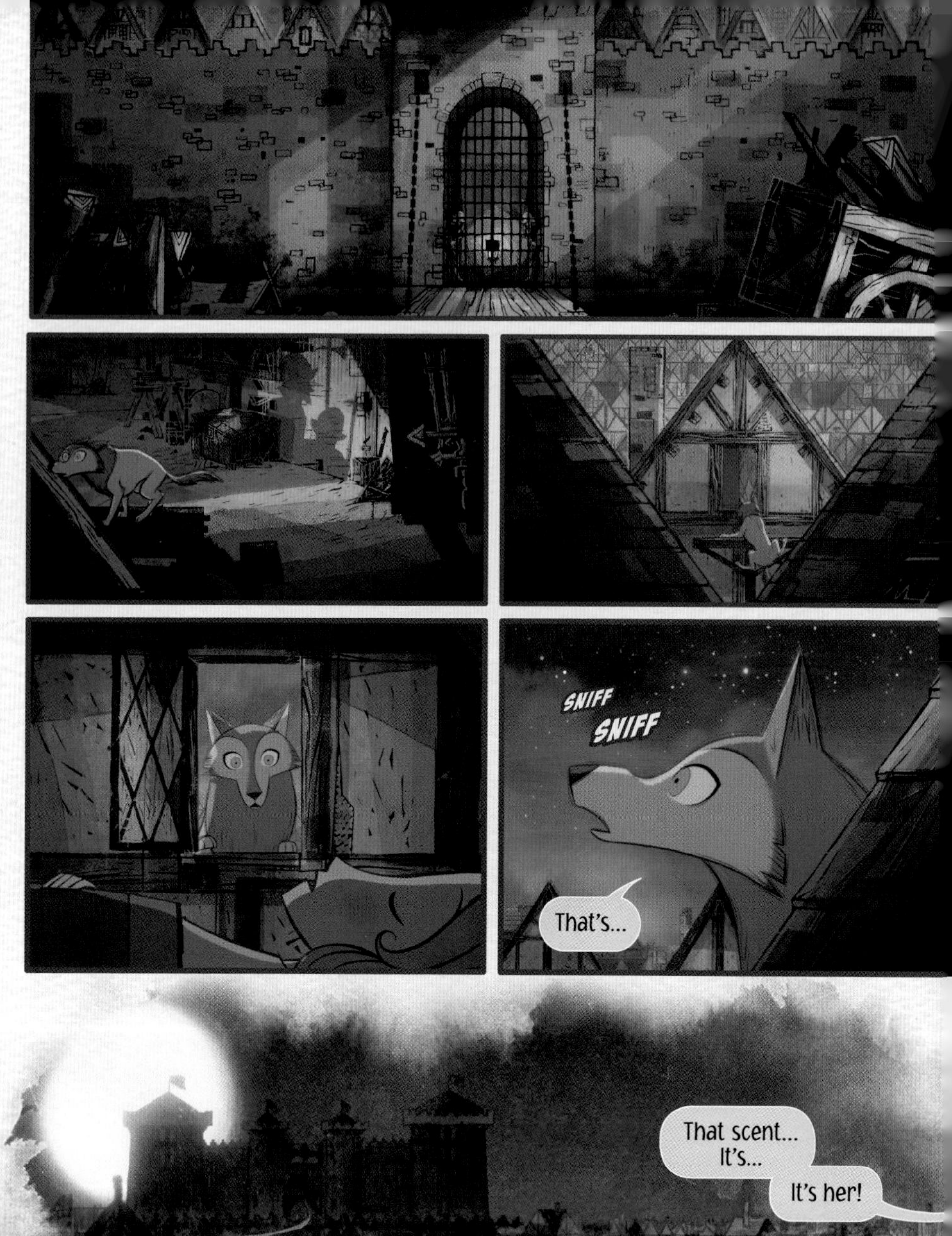
SNIFF
SNIFF
That's...

That scent... It's...
It's her!

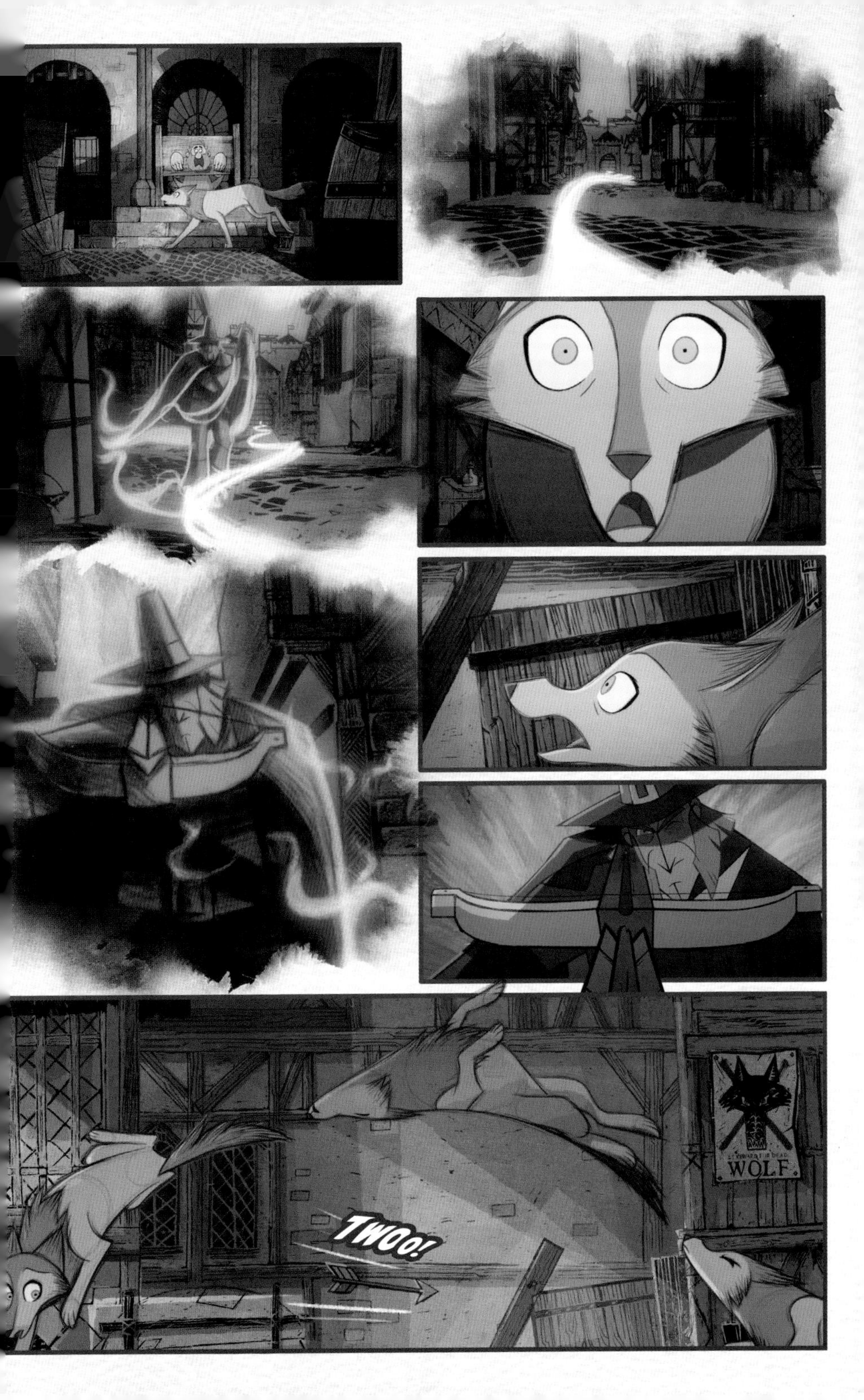
WOLF
TWOo!

TWOO!
Watch out! Whasthadevil?!
Wolf! There's a wolf in here. Get yer young'uns inside!
Quick!
There's a beast goin' around the town, lads. Watch out!
Wolf in the town! WOLF!
The town's goin' mad! MAD, I tell ya!

FWISH
WOLF.
Get it! Now!
Oi, Cromwell! Ye can't stop them! No one can stop them!

I'll handle it, my lord.
Enough... I will deal with this wolf myself.
Back to your beds!

Find that wolf!

Wolf!

That scent...
I knew it!

Girl...Girl...
Here...Quick!
H-hello?
Only a Wolfwalker can make another.
When did it happen to ye? Where? Is the wolf that bit ye near? Is she all right? Is she ***alive? Where is Mebh?!***
Well, she's not a normal wolf. She's...

I know, girl. A normal wolf couldn't have done this to ye.
Where is Mebh? Is she alright? Did she get away?
You're Mebh's mother. Oh, wait till I tell her I found you! She'll be so happy. She's waitin' for you in the forest.
Wolf! Wolf in the castle!
Ye'll be killed like this. Listen, girl. Get back to yer human body right away.
She should never have bitten ye. Get Mebh and leave. Get far away from here, both of ye. It's not safe fer our kind here.
CLICK
CLICK
I can do it, just a little more...

Tell her I'll follow her as soon as I can. But she **must** lead the pack to safety.
Mebh won't leave without you.
CLICK
She must not come fer me. She **must not wait** fer me. She must **run.** And **ye, too, girl.**

Wolves! Do something!
Protect us!
Lord, what must I do? I left to quell rebellion, and now return to more.
This wild land must be civilized. That is your will.

So, wolf...tomorrow I will show them I have tamed you...Just as I will tame this land.
They will have nothing to fear if they trust in the Lord's will.
Go! Tell Mebh to lead the pack to safety! Go! Now!
What the—

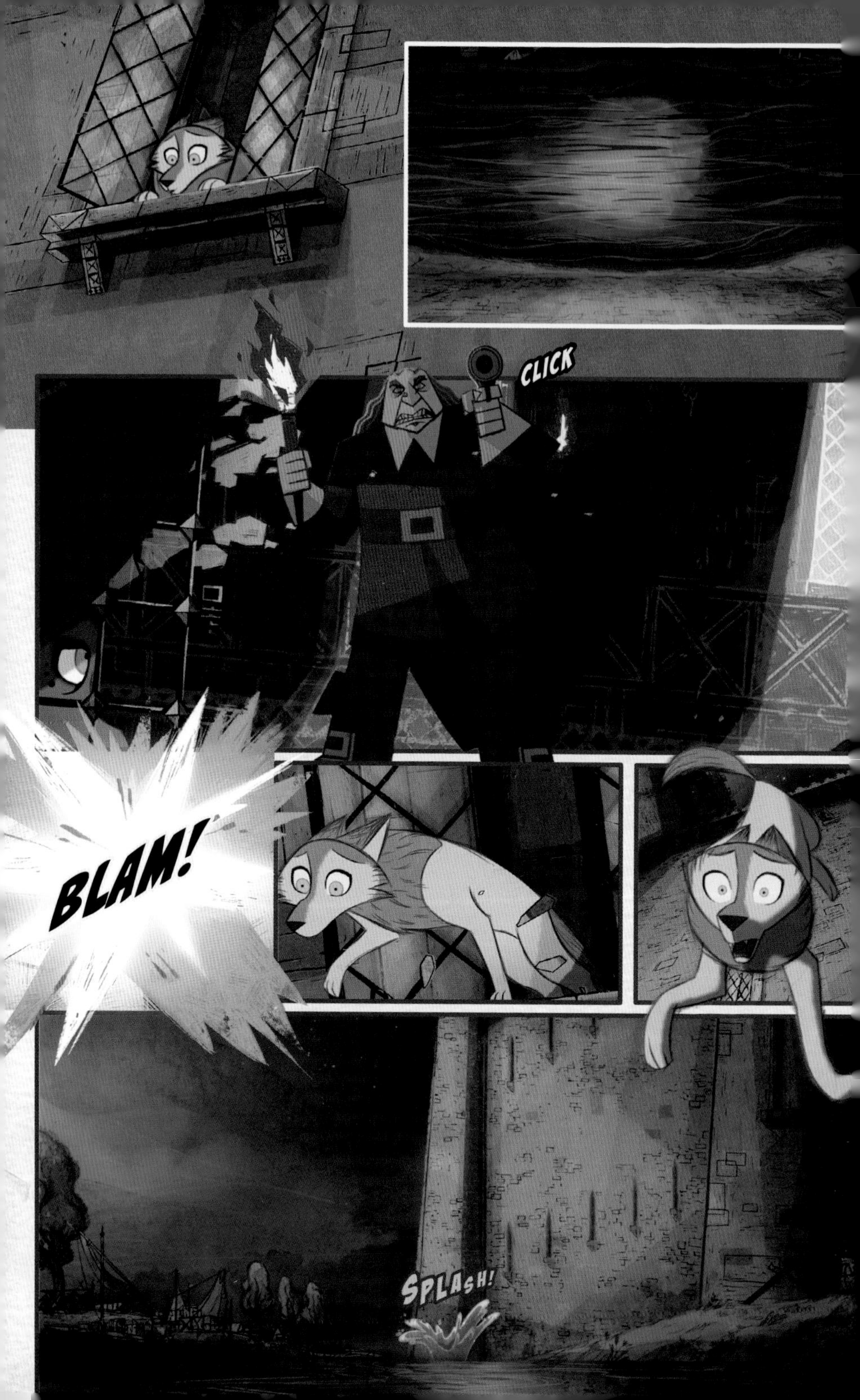

CLICK
BLAM!
SPLASH!

Grrr!
Round up the guards in the square. Immediately!
BLUB GLUB

CREEEEAK
DRIP
DRIP

Oh no! Father!

How do I do this?

Robyn, are you awake?
What, Father?
There was a wolf. Here. In our chambers. It snuck in while you were sleepin'.
It could have taken you.

Father, I...
BANG
BANG
BANG
This world is such a dangerous place for you, lass. I promised I would keep you safe.
But—
Goodfellowe! The Lord Protector wants a word with you.
Goodfellowe!
Sittin' there on yer damn horse...
Goodfellowe. A wolf here...threatening the town. It got inside the castle—in my very chambers!
Wolves runnin' around the town—what are ye doin' about it, Ironsides?! Nathin'!
This is intolerable.

Sir, I—
Enough! You have failed. You are no hunter. From now on, you will serve in my ranks as a foot soldier.
Townspeople! Order, please! Tomorrow I will show you all.
I will tame this land. I will find that den. Every last wolf will be destroyed.
No! Stop! There is another way! Release her—the Wolfwalker.
Please! You must listen!
Take her to the stocks.
NO! SIR! PLEASE! She is just a child!
And I know these woods... I—I can still help on your mission...

Wait.
It's safe now. Go to your beds! Tomorrow I will make good on my word.
GUARDS!
I will give you both one more chance. Follow your orders or you'll be off to war.
Yes, my lord.
And, girl, never speak of such pagan nonsense in this town again. Follow the rules or you will never see your father. Do you understand?
Y-yes, m'lord.
Double the guard. Bar the gates. No more wolves inside these walls.

Listen to me, we must follow our orders if we are to stay together.
You **must** do as you're told, my girl.

Cheep...

GASP!

Made a new friend, Ma. She's a townie...but a nice one.
Her name is Robyn...
She's taller than me, but ***I'm*** stronger. And she brushed me hair and gave me this flower.
And she's from a place called England. And we're gonna meet by the oak tree tomorrow.
And she promised to help. And... and...

SNIFFLE...
Where are ye? Ye promised ye'd come back. But it's been so long now. Are ye lost?
Has somethin' happened to ye?
Robyn will help me find ye, Ma. She promised. There's two of us now....

Mebh...

CAW!

Robyn? Time for work!

Cheep.
Merlyn, I can't get out to Mebh. Find her, tell her to leave. Lead her away. She must go!
Chirp.
At least you can be free....

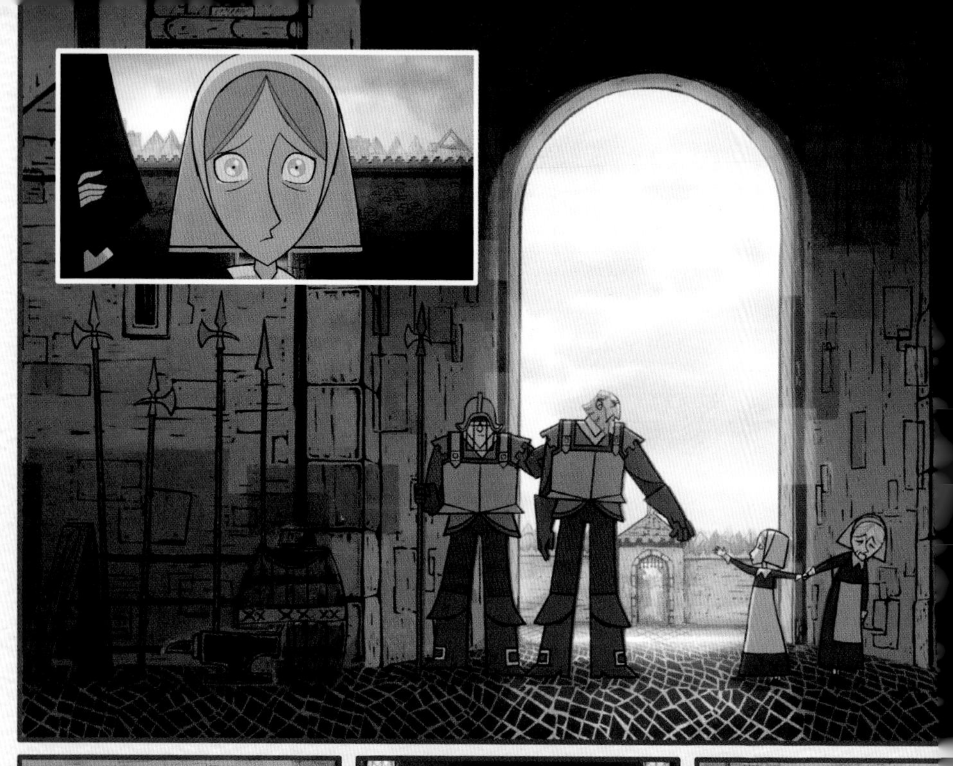

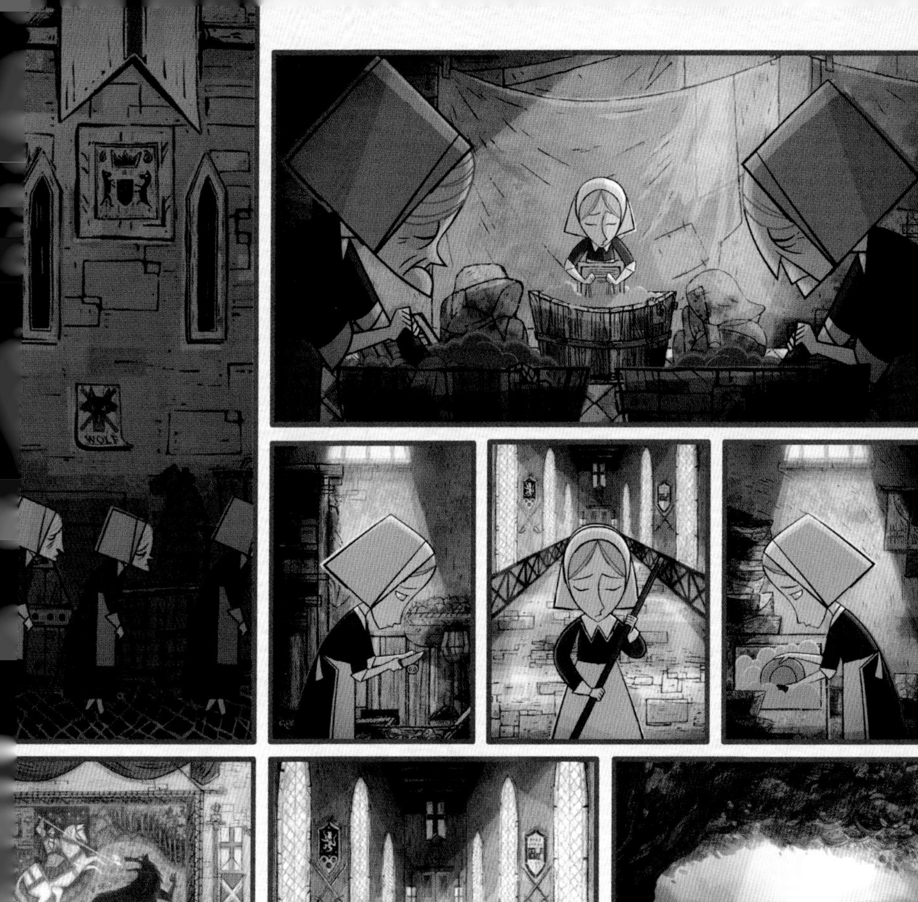
WOLF

Robyn, whats keeping ya?

Birdy!
About time!
Where's Robyn?
Chirp.

What d'ye mean she can't come outta the town?

I'm not leavin'! She promised. Help me find her, Merlyn.

Chirp.

Where were ya?
I waited fer ***ages.***
Mebh! What are you doin' here?

You're supposed to be gone. I sent Merlyn to tell you.

What's that, girl? Who are ye talkin' to?
Oh, nobody...

You must go, Mebh! Lead the pack away to safety.
I told ya! I'm ***not leavin'*** without me ma!

Ye promised!

Mebh, you have to listen to me. You must leave the forest, take the wolves, and go!

Ye promised!
The Lord Protector will **burn** the woods. He will kill **all** the wolves by sunset. You have to get them out.
Do you understand?
Now...**GO!**

Ye said ye would help me...
...Ye **promised!**
Go, Mebh.
Take Merlyn with you.
Goodbye.

I hear he's got a wolf.
The one that was in the town?
A monster.
He's had her fer ages. Locked in the castle. Do ye suppose he's goin' to kill it?! Won't that be a sight?!
Ma!

Hey, watch out, ye mad yolk!
Watch out, girl.
Foolish child! Ye'll hurt someone like that.
Come on now, ladies. Everyone is to go to the courtyard—
They've brought dat big cage outside. 'Tis up on a stage.
What?

Listen to me! I'm the best hunter!
Wolf, wolf, kill the wolf...
Push! Push!

Good, that's enough. Step away. Return to your positions.
What's in the cage?
Look at that, the whole town is here.
Look, they're bringin' a big cage out! What's in the cage?
A big stage, eh? What's he at?
Somethin' to do with the wolf everyone's talkin' about.
Listen, he's talkin' now! What's his plan—he's been promisin' everythin', but we got nothin' so far.
Yeah, a wolf runnin' through the streets—nearly ate me Jimmy.
Me ma's here! Get off of me!
Mebh, ***STOP!*** Please...

People of Kilkenny, I have heard your concerns! Wolf attacks, livestock lost. A wolf running through our very streets.
But have no fear!
Soon this **Wolfland** will be our land. This will be a ***civilized*** country.
Lemme go! Get offa me!
Mebh, stop! You must get out!
Let me go!

Hey! HEY!
Over here! I've caught a wolf!
Let me go! LET ME GO!
Look! She caught a wolf!
My fellow hunters! Looks like we've got a new wolf to kill.
No, no, get offa me, I have to find me ma! Stop it! Get away from me!
I'm gonna eat ye all!

Robyn? What are ye doin'?!

LET ME OUT! I've got to get out!

Mebh! Your mother told me to keep you safe!

Ya liar. Ye knew!

Please! I need me ma!
This is for your own good.

Wolf, wolf, kill the wolf...

Now. Reveal the beast!

Are ye mad, man?
GASP!
Don't open that door, ye loon!

no...
He has got a wolf... look at tha'.
Kill the wolf!
Kill the beast!
Kill it!

Send it to hell!

KILL THE WOLF!!

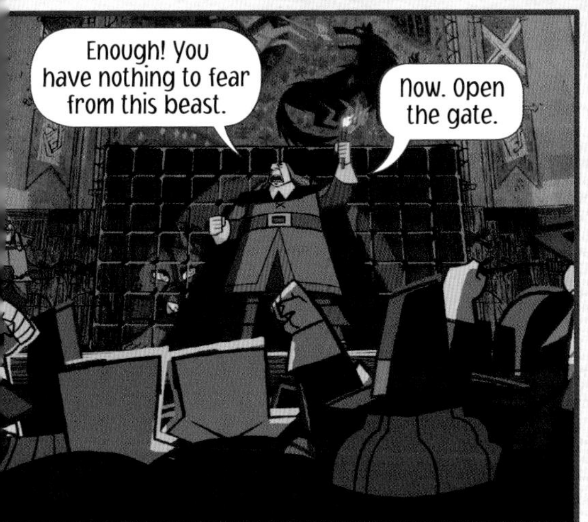
Enough! You have nothing to fear from this beast.
Now. Open the gate.

This once wild creature is now tamed...obedient! A mere faithful servant. I will rid this land of all of its wretched kind.
MA!

Mebh, no!
Hey, watch it!
What's she doin'?
Get off me! Hey!
Huh?
Maaaaa!
Grrrr!
Mebh, no!

Ma! Ma! It's me!
I'm here! Ma!

I'm gonna get ya
out of here, Ma!

What's going
on here?

What the
hell is this?
Look at the
mad girl!
She's gone
wild. Is this part
of the act?
What's she
shoutin' about?
Her mother?

Let her go! That's my ma!
Goodfellowe, take charge of this wild thing.
GRRRRRR
Hah! One girl against all them soldiers. She's winnin' an' all! Go on, girl!
Goodfellowe, can you not catch anything?!

Collar that demon and put her in the stock.
Oh, watch out now! Ye've made her mother angry!

Father!
Don't—
no!
Robyn,
stay back!
Father,
stop! This is
wrong!
Get back!
SNAP
Father!
ARGH!

Aggghhh, the wolf!
Waaagghh, look out!
STOP!

CHOMP!

Pull it back! Pull it back! Lock it up!
The wolf bit him!

Finish this!
GRRRR!

MA!

Watch out!
She's wild!

Hey,
watch it!

Where's
she goin'?!

Ouch!

I am
a Wolfwalker!
I'm gettin' me wolves.
I'm comin' back fer
me ma. Then...

...WE'LL
ATE YE
ALL!
AWWOooo

Huh? A
Wolfwalker?

She's callin' the pack!
AWWOooo
AWWOooo
Bloody hell! Listen to that! It's true! They are comin'!
We are done for!
Do not fear wild girls and wolves.
Because **tonight** we put an end to this. ***I*** will burn this forest to the ground.
I will lead cannons to the den of these beasts and send them all to hell.

Get home!
No!

Lock your doors!
Can't control them wolves.

Prove yourself a worthy soldier tonight or tomorrow you are in ***chains.***

Now, put an end to that wild beast!

What cannot be ***tamed*** must be ***destroyed!***

No, please!... You can't!
Robyn, stop this!
And for goodness sake, put manners on that girl—
Or manners will be put on her.
Enough! Robyn, return to your duties.
No, please! Father, please don't...

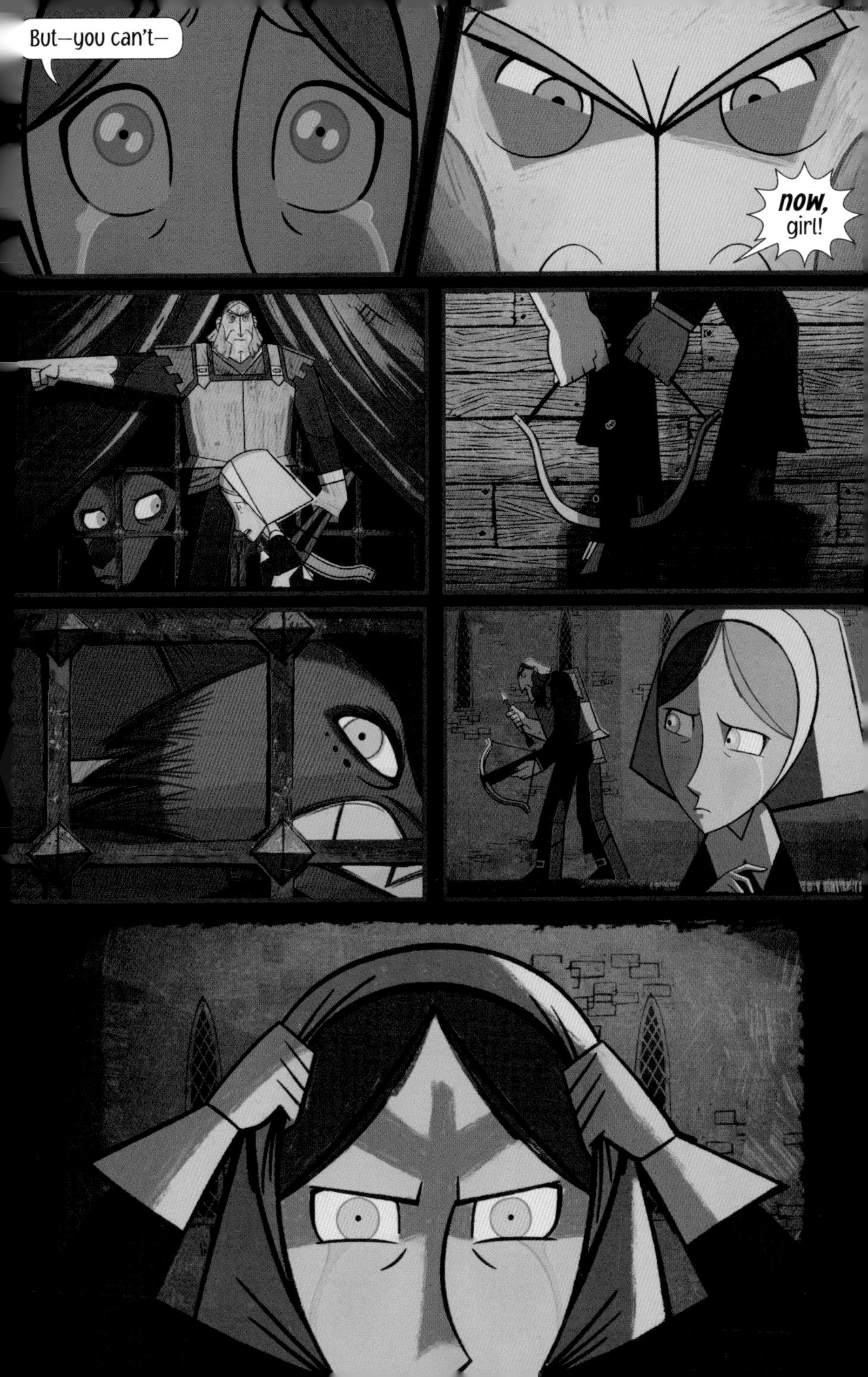
But—you can't—
now, girl!

Robyn!
What are you doin', girl?! The Lord Protector will have us in chains!
He's wrong, Father! All of this is wrong. Don't you see that?
Robyn, step aside! We must do what we're told!
Why, Father? Why?!
Because I'm afraid!

I won't be here to protect you forever. I'm so afraid that one day you'll end up in a cage.

But I already ***am*** in a cage.

D-DONG!

Wolves!
Wolves!

D-DONG!
D-DONG!

What's that?
The alarm is ringin'. Something's wrong out there.
Jaypers, what now?

Wolves! Wolves headin' this way!
Wha!
Quick, get indoors!
Agghh, we're done for! Run!
Get inside, they're comin'!

Wolves are attackin'!

Wolves! Wolves!

Agghh!

I'm sorry, Father.

AGGHH! The wolf, it's out!

Watch out—the beast!

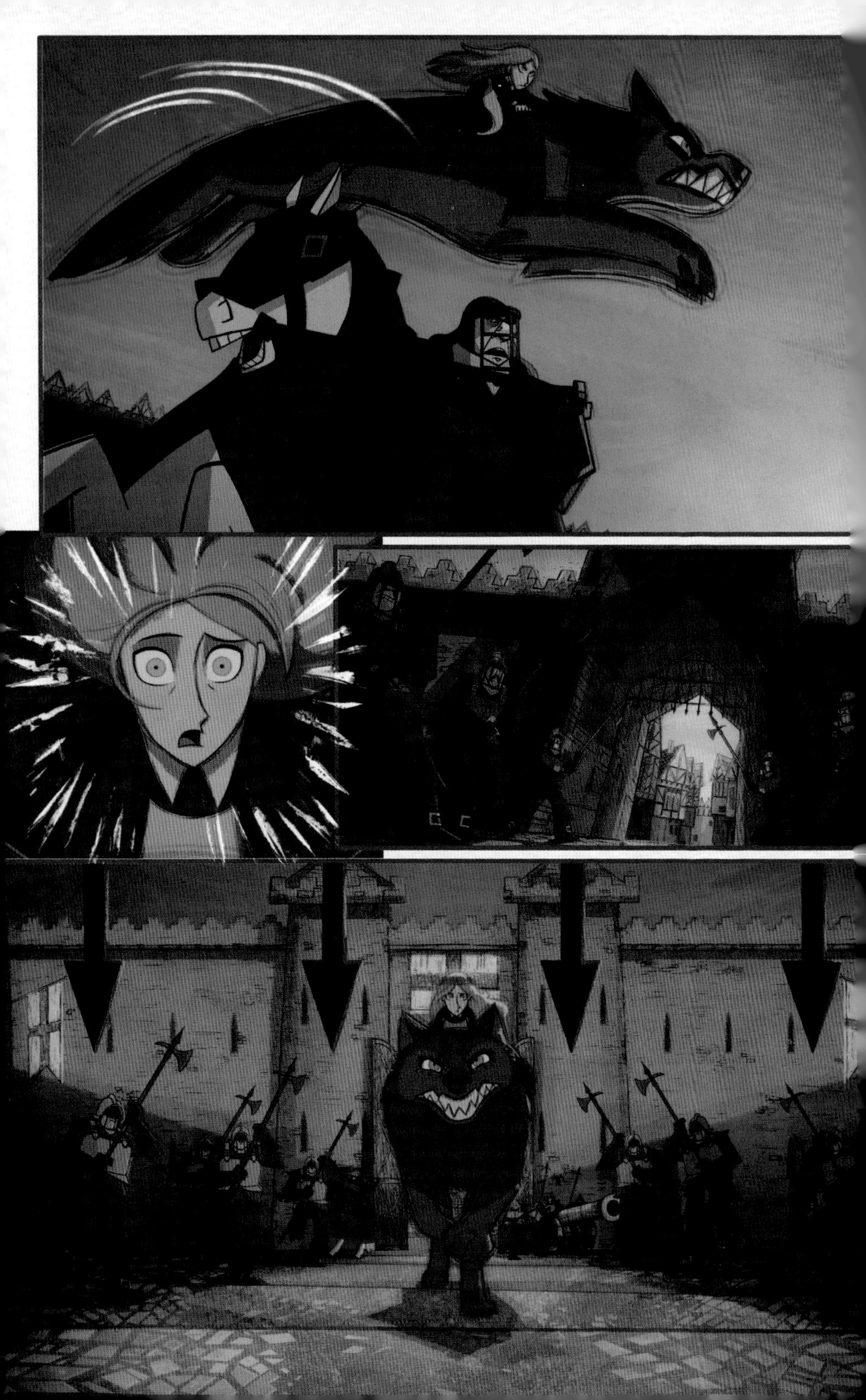

Wolf!
Get it!
Agghhh—
Ma, help me!
Kill it!
Wahoo!
Go on, girl.
It's headin' fer the gate!
I tried to stop her. But I failed.
She's goin' to get herself *killed.*
Close the gate!
Raise the drawbridge!

Fire!
BANG!
BANG!
Woolllff!
Noo!
POW
POW
POW
BOOM!

AWWOooo
It's time fer us to attack those townies! Let's ate them all!
They...
Have my...
Ma...

Ma.
Mebh, love...
Ma, yer back!
I thought I would never see ye again.
Until this one freed me.

Mebh...I'm so sorry.
I was only tryin' to keep you safe... Tryin' to help...
I—I didn't know what to do... I was...I'm sorry, Mebh.
Ahh, shut up, townie. Haha. Thanks fer helpin' Ma.
I'm not a townie anymore, Mebh.
Mebh, we don't have much time.
The Lord Protector is leadin' an army out, and he's—
FFFT!
THUMP!
AHHHH! NO, MA! NO!

Ma! What happened t' ye?! Don't leave me again. Wake up, Ma. Please. ***PLEASE!***
Robyn, run! Quick!
No, Father. What have you done?!

Stop! Let me go! Mebh!
Back!
Father! You—you shot her!
Back, stay back!

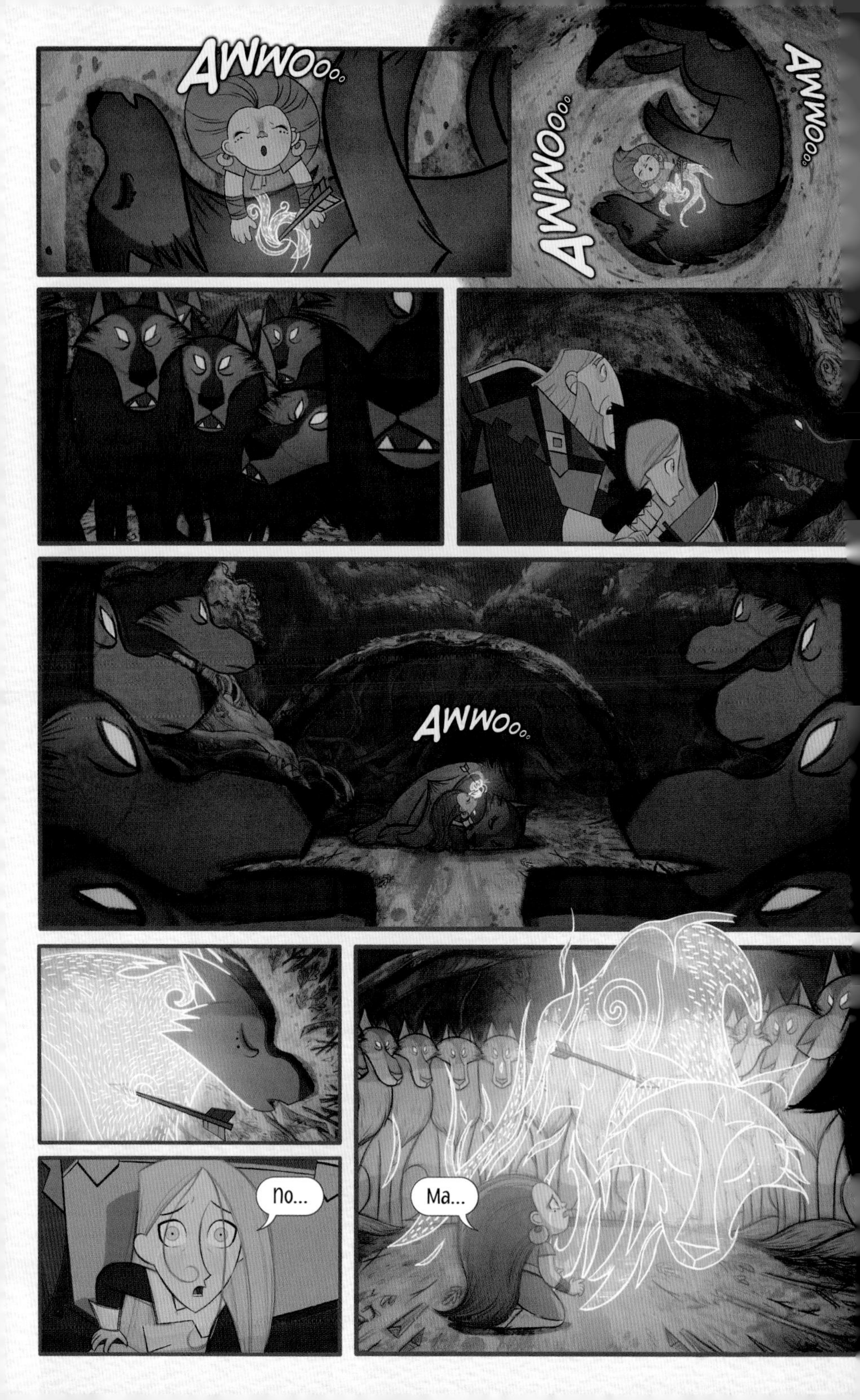
AWWOooo
AWWOooo
AWWOooo
AWWOooo
no...
Ma...

Robyn, no. Stay.
No, Father! Let me go! ***I have to help her...*** She's dyin'. I have to go with them.

No, Robyn, ***why?!*** I don't understand!

Don't you see? I'm one of them.
I'm a Wolfwalker.

No, Robyn. Please...
I can't let you go.

Father...

VHMMMM

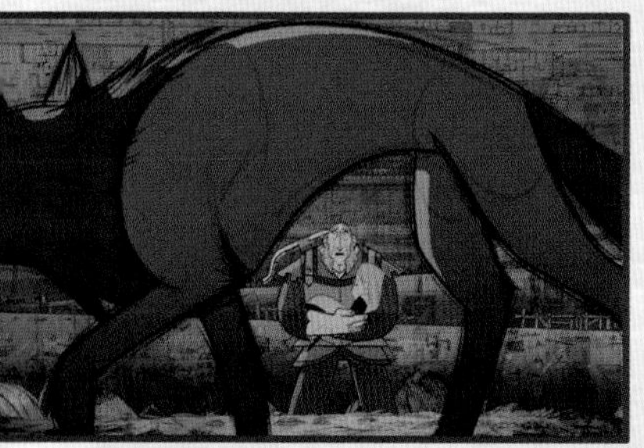

Robyn! ROBYN!

Goodfellowe, have you lost your senses? What is going on here?
Robyn...She... She's gone....

Chain him. We'll deal with him later.

SNAP!
A fresh track. Move on!
Burn it all!

Oh God, what have I done? Robyn, wake up. Please. Please.

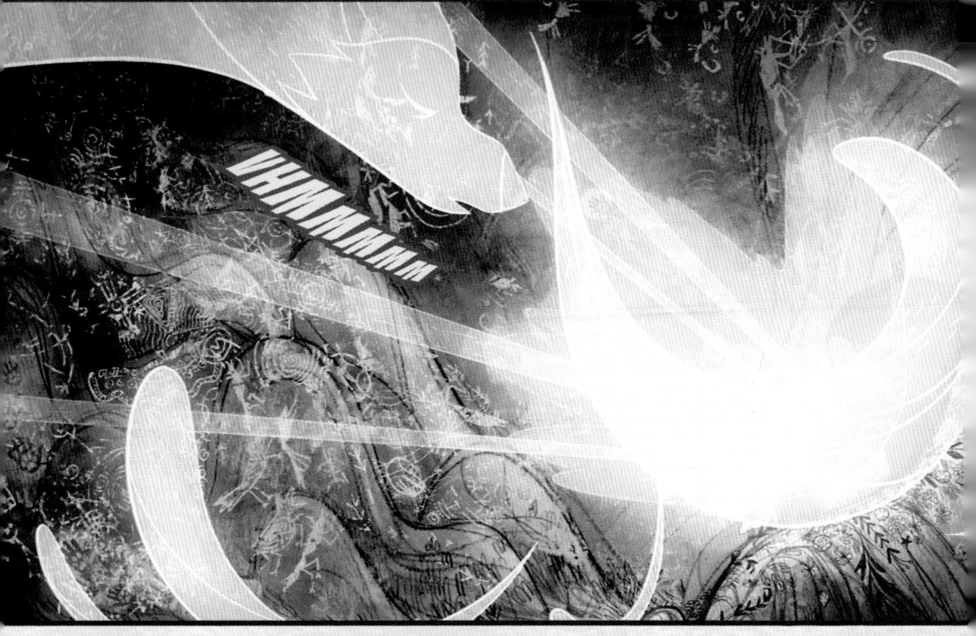
VHMMMMMM

Ma!

Please, Ma,
breathe...

I never healed
anythin' this bad
before. It's gonna
take time.

I'm not
leavin'
ya, Ma.

KABOOM!

I'll hold them off.
Wolves, follow her!

KABOOM!
They're in there! Advance!

We can drive them back! We're *wolves!*
They have guns...
...a cannon...
...but don't be afraid.
They are in *our* forest.

Take cover in the trees.
"Draw their fire—"
"Then strike from the shadows when they're reloadin'. Use the traps!"

There's something out here, m'lord!
Load your weapons. Fan out!
VHMMMM

SNAP!
AAAAAAA!!
BANG!
AAAAAAA!!
REPORT!

I can't, Ma, ***I can't.*** I'm not strong enough.

Please... tell me what to do.

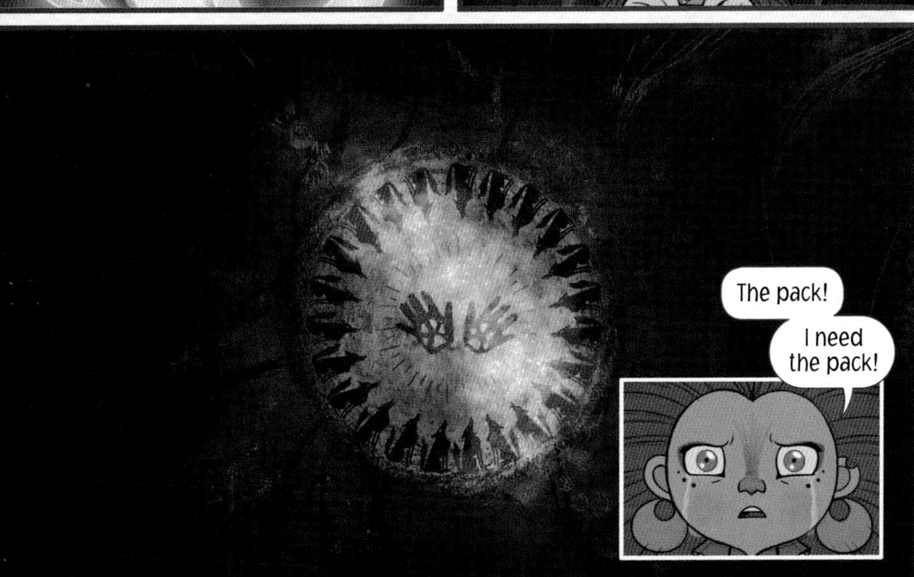
The pack!
I need the pack!

SNAP!
GRRRR!

AWWOooo

That wild girl is calling them!
We ain't got a chance.
It's a Wolfwalker!

AWWOOooo

Witchcraft!
What the—?

It ain't natural!
That's not normal wolves, sir, we're gone!
What do you think you're doing?! Get back to your positions!
RUN!
Cowards!

The stories are true!
The wolves!
Ooof!
We're surrounded!
BANG
BANG
Get out of here! Run!

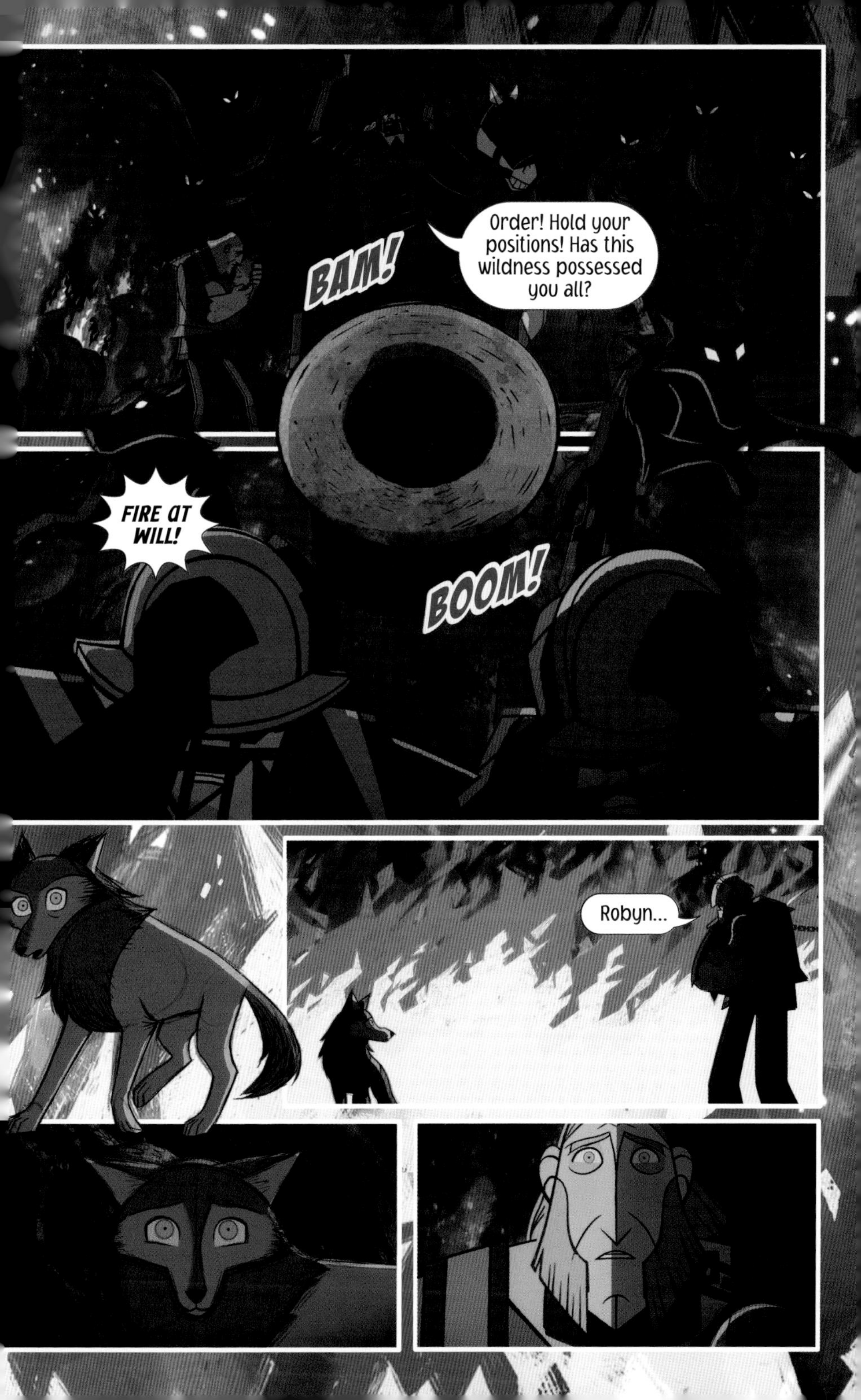
BAM!
Order! Hold your positions! Has this wildness possessed you all?
FIRE AT WILL!
BOOM!
Robyn...

BANG
Robyn, GO!
Onward!

Don't let them get away!
Gunners! Slay the foul beasts!
BABOOM!
KRAKASH!
Quick, everyone! Down here! I need yer help!

Robyn...!

Where's Robyn?!

AWWOooo
Men, run and **you will be killed!** Follow my will, and we **will** prevail. The **Lord** is guiding us.

Hurry with that weapon. Our victory is at hand!

AWWOOoo
Robyn?
Robyn!

SHOW YOURSELVES, YOU WICKED CREATURES! COME MEET YOUR END!

There's the devil's lair! Load the cannon!

Musketeers...!
Robyn...!

Fire!
No!

No!
Robyn!
BANG

BAM! BANG

It ain't natural!
Run!
Get back here!
THUNK!
KRAKOOM!

Robyn.
Robyn.

Robyn, get up. Run!
Enough, Goodfellowe.
CHEEEEEP!
Skree!
Aggh! Foul bird!
CLANK

Stop, she's just a girl!
ROBYN! NO!

By God's glory and punishment, he vanquishes thee.
WHAM!
GRRRRRRRR!

Lord, protect me...
Cheep!

CRUNCH

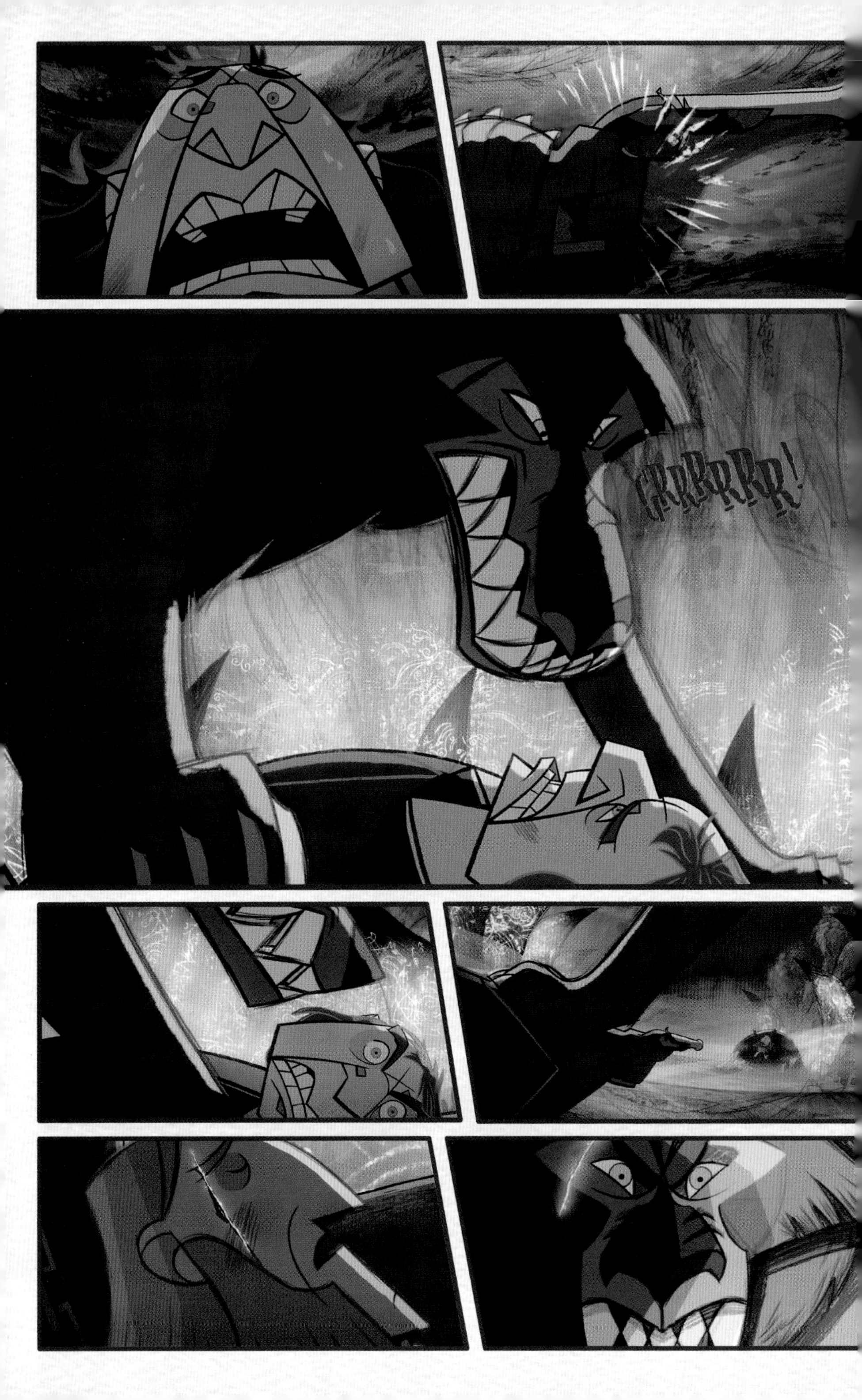
GRRRRRR!

Goodfellowe!
PTANG!

CRNCHCH

CLICK
Into your arms, my Lord...

Father, you're one of us now.

AWWOooo

We have to help Mebh.

Please, Ma, don't go. Don't go. Don't leave me again....

Like I promised...
There's two of us now.
Yeh...There's
two of us.
Follow me...

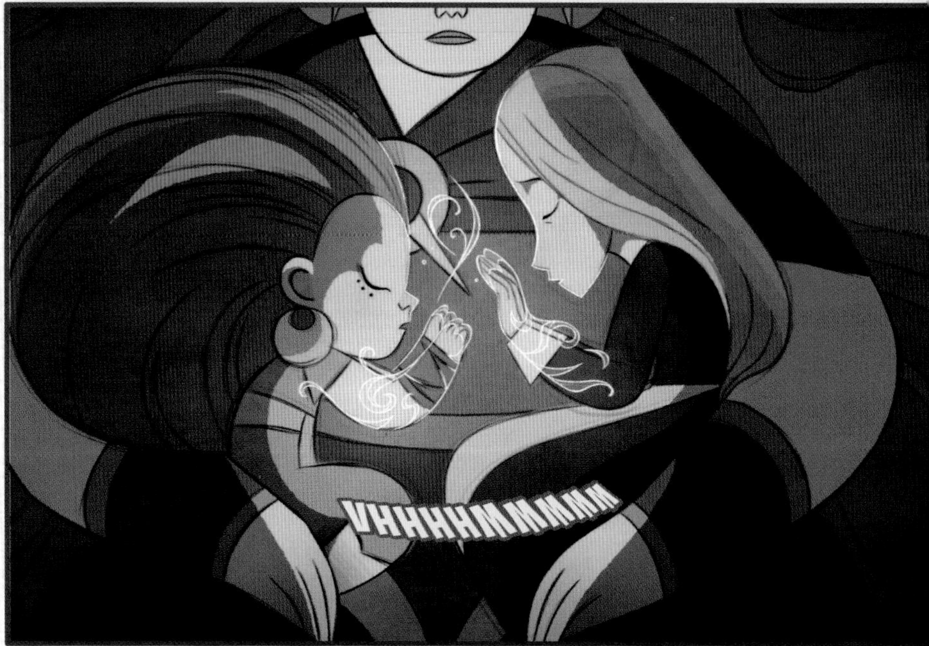
VHHHHMMMMM

AWWOooo

AWWOooo

AWWOooo

AWWOoooo
'Tis lovely music.

AWWOOoo
Mebh...
Ma... MaMa
MaMa MaMa...

Haha!

Thank ye, *mo chara...* ***My friend.***

Father?

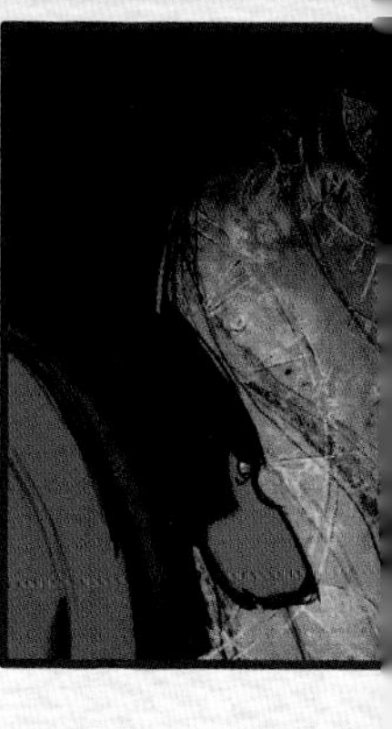

Stay...Please.
Yer one of us.

Father... You're in our pack now.

All is well, my love.
All is well, Father.

Come on!
Race ya!

The wolf will run
Till risin' sun.

The wolf will leap
from child asleep.

Wolf, wolf,
Howls the wolf!

Run free over
and under!

Wolf, wolf
Howls the wolf
For ever and ever
and after!

Dylan Vaughan

Tomm Moore is the cofounder and Creative Director of Cartoon Saloon. Tomm directed *The Secret of the Kells* and *Song of the Sea*, both nominated for the Academy Award for Best Animated Feature.

Ross Stewart has been painting, illustrating, designing, and working in animation for over twenty years. Ross has worked on three Oscar nominated movies: *The Secret of the Kells* (Art Director), *Song of the Sea* (concept artist), and *ParaNorman* (visual development). He has also illustrated books and literature for a variety of publishers. He is a nature lover and would gladly sit under an oak tree all day long.

Tomm and Ross codirected *WolfWalkers*, their latest feature film.

Anna Stark

Samuel Sattin is a writer and coffee addict. He is the words behind the Glint trilogy, *Bezkamp*, *Legend*, and *The Silent End*. His work has appeared or been featured in *The Nib*, *The Atlantic*, NPR, and elsewhere. He holds an MFA in Comics from California College of the Arts and has a creative writing MFA from Mills College. Residing in Oakland, California, he sometimes teaches at the California College of the Arts and lives with his wife/assassin and two cats.

Acknowledgments

As a fan of graphic novels from an early age, the visual language of the medium has been a part of my work as a director since the beginning. For *WolfWalkers,* Ross and I drew inspiration from many of our favorite creators and even incorporated graphic novel–style compositions and scene layouts into the film itself, so it was especially exciting for me to be part of adapting our film to the page. We even added some original pages detailing the movie's backstory and the legend of the Wolfwalkers as a bonus to the readers.

I would like to dedicate this graphic novel to the amazing crew who worked with us on the animated feature *WolfWalkers* since so much of their artwork is the basis of everything you will see in the book. I would also like to thank Megan, Rachel, and everyone at Little, Brown Books for Young Readers for their patience and enthusiasm for this adaptation, especially Ching, who made such beautiful layouts and did such a wonderful job designing the book.

Not forgetting, of course, special thanks are due to Sam Sattin, who has done such an excellent job of adapting the script and film for this graphic novel and our team in the Saloon: Desirée, Brian, and especially Maria, who was the not only super fast on the adaptation pages and the original artwork we created for this book but is also one of the most talented artists with whom I've had the pleasure of collaborating.

—Tomm Moore

WolfWalkers

The Graphic Novel